PROMISE OF THE WITCH

WITCHES OF KEATING HOLLOW
BOOK THIRTEEN

DEANNA CHASE

ABOUT THIS BOOK

After ditching her cheating boyfriend, Zya Rossi left Salem and all her meddling ancestors for a fresh start in Keating Hollow. While she managed to lose the boyfriend, unfortunately her ancestors followed her. While her dead aunts are trying to set her up with every eligible bachelor, Zya is just trying to make friends. She's not interested in dating anyone. But when her best friend shows up on her doorstep with his three-year-old daughter in tow, suddenly she finds herself battling old feelings and trying not to fall in love with the one man she can't afford to lose.

Brody Saxon spent the last five years in France, using his magic to cultivate award winning grapes for an up and coming winery. Having never been the commitment type, after spending his days in the vineyards, he'd been quite content to spend his nights playing the field. But his carefree lifestyle comes crashing down when he suddenly finds himself the sole guardian of a daughter he hadn't even known he'd had. Now he's in Keating Hollow, on Zya's doorstep, praying his best friend can help him make sense of his new life. And maybe finally face the fact that he's been in love with her for years. The problem? They're both runners. Finding a way to trust each other is proving to be more of a challenge than getting his three-year-old to sleep in her own bed.

CHAPTER 1

*D*aughter, Zya thought to herself as she watched her oldest and dearest friend tenderly sweep a black curl out of the young girl's eye.

Brody Saxon had a daughter.

Zya still couldn't believe it. In fact, she wasn't at all sure she wasn't dreaming. Surely she'd wake up soon and find out Brody hadn't just shown up on her front steps. That he was still in France, living the bachelor life while taking the wine industry by storm.

"Goodnight, sweet girl," Brody whispered to Winnie and then gave her a kiss on the cheek.

She blinked up sleepily at him and in a tiny, exhausted voice said, "I need PJ."

Brody glanced at the backpack at his feet, his face stricken with panic. "I'm sure the puppy is here somewhere."

Zya walked over to the open suitcase and picked up the green-and-purple stuffed puppy. She cleared her throat, getting Brody's attention.

Relief flashed in his brilliant blue eyes as he held his hand out for the stuffed toy. He mouthed, *Thank you.*

Nodding to him, she turned and walked out of the spare room, down the hall, and into her kitchen, where she made a pot of coffee and refilled her cat's water and food dishes. Lyra, the pure white cat, appeared from under the table, rubbing Zya's calf with her head before she settled in for her dinner. While the coffee brewed, Zya pulled out the box of half-eaten coffee cake from Incantation Café and then sat at the table and waited.

When Brody finally appeared and sat across from her, he dropped his head into his hands and groaned.

"That sounds ominous," Zya said as she got up and poured him a cup of coffee. When she placed it in front of him, she asked, "Is this good, or do you need something a little stronger?"

Brody eyed the mug. "You wouldn't have any Irish cream, would you?"

Without a word, she went to her fridge and retrieved the bottle. After giving them each a generous pour into their cups, she replaced it and took her seat.

"Thank you." He took a long sip.

"For the booze? Or are you relieved I haven't ripped you a new one yet?"

He let out a humorous chuckle. "Both." Sitting back in his chair, he finally lifted his gaze to hers and said, "I still can't believe this is real."

Zya reached across the table and squeezed his hand. "I'm so sorry. Losing Colette must have come as a real shock."

He blinked at her. "Colette? What does this have to do with Colette?"

"I..." Zya shook her head, confused. "You said Winnie is

three and a half years old. I just assumed that Colette is her mother." Colette was the woman he'd followed to France five years ago. They'd broken up about a year after he moved there, but he'd stayed because he had a dream job at a winery.

"Oh, right." He grimaced and he lowered his gaze so that he didn't meet her eyes. "Colette and I were more off than on the last six months, and in the off months I wasn't exactly a monk."

"So Winnie is the product of a one-night stand?" she asked, reading between the lines.

He closed his eyes and nodded, looking miserable. "Her mother died in a car accident about six weeks ago."

Sympathy for Winnie overwhelmed her. She couldn't imagine what it would be like to lose a mother at such a young age. And then to have her entire life, everything she'd known, uprooted as she moved to another country meant that Winnie's entire existence had been turned upside down. The poor sweet baby. Zya wanted to walk back into the guest room where the little girl slept and just hold her and make sure she knew there were people on this earth that cared about her. That no matter what, her mother would never be forgotten.

She ordered herself to stay seated. Winnie didn't even know Zya. The last thing she needed was some strange woman trying to comfort her. Brody was the one she trusted. The one who needed to be there for his little girl. Zya had always had a hard time imagining Brody as a father, but now that she'd witnessed him with Winnie, she just knew that there was nothing he wouldn't do for her.

Turning her attention to the father in question, Zya stared at him and couldn't help the hurt that pierced her heart. She still wasn't able to process the fact that he'd kept his daughter a secret from her. She'd thought he was her best friend. There was no way on the goddess's green earth that she'd ever keep something like that from him. "Winnie is the reason you stayed in France," she said almost to herself.

Brody's head jerked up suddenly. "What? No. Zya, I didn't even know about her until I got the call that Lucie had passed."

Shock filtered down Zya's spine, rendering her speechless. She blinked at her friend and then the fury set in. "You mean you had a daughter and the mother didn't *tell* you about her?"

He nodded. "That's right. I don't know why. I could make some guesses, but that's all they'd be. Her parents died in the same car accident, leaving Winnie with no family. Lucie did name me in a very simple will. She left the care of her daughter to me along with a copy of the birth certificate." He cupped the back of his neck. "Lucie never told me, but she at least wrote it down for the lawyers in case anything happened to her."

"That means you've had Winnie for six weeks now?" Zya asked, trying to recover from the bombshell he'd just dropped.

"Almost. It took a few days for everything to get worked out. It's been…" He shook his head. "I hired a nanny, but that didn't go well. Winnie couldn't adjust and my job was too demanding. I was leaving early all the time, refusing to travel, and unable to give the winery my every waking moment like I used to. They weren't happy. I wasn't happy. And Winnie certainly wasn't. So I packed everything and just came home."

"How long were you in Salem?" she asked, not wanting to bring up his parents. They lived there, but they weren't the easiest people to deal with. She could only imagine how they took the news of finding out they had a grandchild that no one had told them about.

"Three days."

The words were said with a finality that told Zya he wouldn't be elaborating. But she had to ask anyway. "Do you want to talk about it?"

He shook his head. "It was as bad as you might imagine. I just... it wasn't a good environment for Winnie."

Zya knew his parents well. She could only imagine that Brody's mother had tried to take over completely while ignoring anything Brody might have wanted for his daughter. She also figured his dad had lectured him on his irresponsibility and how he'd always known Brody would be a disappointment. The Saxons ran with the elite crowd of Salem, and their reputation meant more to them than just about anything. If they became the talk of the country club, it would be a huge scandal. She cleared her throat. "So, Keating Hollow it is then?"

Brody took another long sip of his spiked coffee and nodded as a small smile claimed his lips. It was the first time she'd seen anything other than weariness on his handsome face. "It appears so."

Zya returned his smile as she gazed at the handsome man sitting across from her. He needed a shave and his dark wavy hair was mussed from a long day of travel, but his sapphire eyes were shining at her, making her practically melt right there in her kitchen. It wasn't just because he was so good looking. Though that helped. It was the fact that he'd come to her when he needed a safe place to land. "I'm glad you're here."

"Me, too, Zya. Me, too." He leaned back in the chair and let out a long breath as the tension seemed to just drain from him. "Thanks for letting us stay here tonight. Tomorrow I'll start looking at what's available."

Zya frowned. "What? Why?" She waved a hand around at her rambling ranch home. It was larger than Zya needed, but she'd purchased it because it was situated in the woods with a lake view and had easily accessible trails that she made use of regularly. "You and Winnie can stay here. There's plenty of room. It's just me and Lyra."

"That's sweet, Zya. I love that you offered, but I can't ask you to live with a three-year-old," he said, squeezing her hand. "I'm betting your cat won't be a fan either."

She stared at him, confused. "Live with? How long are you staying here in Keating Hollow?"

He frowned, matching her confused expression. "Didn't I already tell you?"

"Tell me what?" she asked, getting impatient.

"We're moving here." He let out a soft chuckle. "One of my contacts in the industry hooked me up with the Pelsh winery. I'm starting there next week."

Zya's entire body deflated. Brody hadn't come to Keating Hollow for her. He hadn't called her when he learned about Winnie. He hadn't even told her he was moving back to the States. He'd only shown up on her doorstep because he'd been offered a job in her new town. Bristling, she pulled her hand out of his and grabbed the two empty coffee mugs. "I see. You're saying it was just a coincidence that I happened to live here, then."

"Well, yeah. A happy one, wouldn't you say?"

"Sure, Brody." She forced a smile and pointed at the coffee cake. "You should eat that. You've got to be hungry."

Brody stood and followed her over to the sink. "Zy?"

She didn't answer as she rinsed the mugs and put them in her dishwasher.

"Zy," he said again, more insistent.

"What is it, Brody?" she asked, staring out her window at the moonlight shimmering over the small lake.

"You're mad at me." It was a statement, not a question.

She clenched her jaw and took in a deep breath, trying to

settle herself. "I never said I was mad," she said. "It's just... I don't know." Zya turned to look at him. "I'm disappointed, I guess. You've had a lot going on and I didn't know about any of it until you showed up unannounced."

"I'm sorry. It's been a really rough time and I thought if I called you..." He swallowed hard and then shook his head before he whispered, "Please don't be upset. I couldn't stand it if you're mad at me, too." He seemed so vulnerable, almost broken as he said the words.

All of Zya's disappointment vanished as she wrapped her arms around him and pulled him in for a hug. She'd never seen him look so raw before, and all she wanted to do was wrap him in her arms and hold his broken pieces together. Brody had been her best friend since they were kids. She *knew* him. He was struggling.

Shame replaced all her disappointment and hurt that he hadn't told her about Winnie. That he hadn't made a point of calling her. Was it such a huge surprise that he hadn't? Brody was never one for regular phone calls before anyway. It was a quick text or email with the occasional call, usually when she initiated it. He had a child to care for now, and his entire life had been sent into a tailspin. Her job was to be there for him, not force him to soothe her bruised ego.

He might have come to Keating Hollow for a job, but that didn't mean he didn't need her support. He'd come to her the moment he'd arrived in town, hadn't he? She'd be damned if she let him down now. "I'm not mad," she said again, this time in a soft voice. "And even if I was, I never could stay mad at you."

He gripped her tightly and then chuckled. "It's because of my boyish charm."

"It's because I feel sorry for you," she teased. "Such a sad case. It's too bad you're such an ugly duckling. If it weren't for your crooked nose and that horrid case of adult acne, you might actually be sort of cute."

He pulled back and grinned at her, flashing her his devastating smile, the one that made her go weak in the knees. "Cute, huh? I guess there's hope after all."

Zya's gaze dropped to his lips as butterflies fluttered in her stomach. It was one of the many moments when she was reminded that she loved him. That she'd always loved him. And that she likely always would.

Best friends, she told herself. That's all they were. And Zya wasn't going to do anything to jeopardize what they had. Tearing her eyes away from his lips, she took a step back and smirked at him. Patting his shoulder, she said, "It's always sad when the fives think they're a ten. The sooner you accept your lot in life, the easier it will be."

His eyes twinkled as he let out a loud laugh.

She couldn't help it. She laughed with him.

"Zy?"

"Yeah?"

"Thanks. I needed that."

CHAPTER 2

*B*rody watched as Zya walked out of the kitchen and down the hall toward her bedroom. There was a time in his life when all he'd wanted to do was follow her. He'd actually done it once when they were in college, but just as he'd turned the corner to her dorm room, he'd spotted her tugging some nerdy, literary type into her room. He'd waited a few minutes, hoping she'd kick him out, but she never did and he'd spent the rest of the evening trying to get the image of his hot best friend and the nerdy dude out of his mind.

He'd tried hooking up with a pretty blond cheerleader, but when that went south, he'd moved on to a half bottle of tequila. That had done the trick... at least until he'd spent the entire next day puking his guts out.

Groaning, Brody ran a hand through his thick hair and tugged until it stung.

He needed to stop thinking about Zya as if she was hookup material. He'd done that far too often over the years, but if there was one person he couldn't go there with, it was her. She was his person. The one he counted on. Even if he hadn't told her about Winnie. He'd just been too overwhelmed and unready to face her. And the truth was, he'd been afraid if he opened himself up to her that he'd have broken down completely. That wasn't something he could risk. He'd had to hold it together. For Winnie.

There was no doubt that she'd have been there for him from the start. Zya was the one person he could always count on no matter what. He knew that without a doubt, and it's why he couldn't cross that line in their relationship.

Brody knew we was terrible when it came to romantic relationships. The longest he'd stayed with anyone had been Collette, and even that had been up and down. More down than up, and now he had a daughter to prove it. But his relationship with Zya? It was the only constant he had in his life. He couldn't mess that up. He wouldn't. Not for a night of pleasure. He had too much to lose.

After checking on his daughter one more time and finding her fast asleep with the cat at the end of her bed, he slipped into the guest room next to hers and crashed out in minutes, dreaming about a tall, gorgeous brunette who never missed an opportunity to bust his balls.

BRODY STOOD at Zya's kitchen window, sipping a fresh cup of coffee and praying the caffeine would put a dent in his massive jetlag. It had been a long haul to get to Salem from France. Then the three days at his parents' house had been pure hell. Resting hadn't been in the cards for either him or Winnie. Not with his mother melting down on him about how irresponsible he was and that his actions had caused her to miss over three years of her granddaughter's life.

As if it had been his fault that Lucie hadn't told him about her. Anger burned deep in his gut as it always did these days when he thought about Lucie and her choices. And worse, now she was gone and there weren't any answers. He'd never know exactly why she chose to keep Winnie a secret; all he could do was guess. Guilt spread like wildfire, extinguishing his tumultuous emotions. How could he be angry at someone who'd died?

He blinked his blurry eyes and squinted at the movement near the lake off in the distance behind Zya's house. His best friend walked along her property line along with a snow-white wolf. The pair seemed so serene in the morning twilight. Ethereal.

Brody's heart ached a little as he took in her beauty, both body and soul.

"Daddy?" Winnie said in a small voice from behind him.

He spun around and moved toward his daughter, crouching down to her level. "Hey, baby girl. How did you sleep?"

She rubbed at her big blue eyes. "Okay. I'm hungry."

"Let's see what Auntie Zya has, okay?" He took her by the hand and together, they stared into the fridge, looking for something she might like for breakfast.

"Pancakes," she said.

He grinned. "Pancakes were my favorite as a kid, too." After getting Winnie set up at the table with a cup of milk, he rummaged around in Zya's fridge and cabinets until he found everything he needed to get started. By the time Zya walked in the back door, he had a stack of pancakes ready to go.

"Whoa," Zya said, eyeing the kitchen. "What's going on in here?"

"Exactly what it looks like," Brody said as he squirted some whipped cream onto a pancake. "I didn't find any syrup, but we raided your whipped cream and blackberry jam."

She peered at the pancake that had a face painted on it with blackberry jam and whipped cream hair. "That's creative."

"Pancakes!" Winnie said, holding her hands out toward Brody.

Brody handed the plate to Zya. "You heard the woman. She wants her pancakes."

Zya chuckled and took the plate over to the child. "Here you go, sweetie."

Winnie promptly swiped her hand through the jam and whipped cream before smearing it over her face as she tried to lick the sugary goodness off her fingers.

"Wow," Zya said, laughing as she met Brody's gaze.

He chuckled, realizing that six weeks ago, he would have been horrified by the scene in front of him. But after being thrown into the deep end of parenting, he'd adjusted rather quickly and now just found it amusing.

"You know," Zya said thoughtfully. "When I got your text last night, I sort of imagined that we'd be hungover and desperate for someone else to cook us breakfast this morning. Yet, here you are with a spatula in your hand. I dare say, this might even be better."

Brody held her gaze as something inside of his chest shifted. It was just a twinge, but it left him feeling raw and a little unsteady on his feet. He cleared his throat. "You always were one for trying to get someone else to handle the kitchen duties."

"That's a lie and you know it," she said with a chuckle.

"Is it though?" He eyed her, calling her bluff. Zya was a very good cook. He'd never deny that. But she liked to cook as a hobby when she was in the mood, not as a daily chore.

She shrugged one shoulder and moved to the counter to plate both of them their own pancakes. Together, they joined Winnie at the table and dug in.

"Oh. Em. Gee, Brody," Zya said. "What did you put in these? They are delicious."

"Nutmeg and vanilla," he said.

"No way. There's something more in there." She closed her eyes and let out a small moan of pleasure.

Brody shifted in his seat, trying to ignore the rush of heat that made every last one of his nerves tingle. Damn that was sexy.

Her eyes popped open and she stared at him expectantly. "Give it up, Saxon," she ordered. "Why do these pancakes taste like heaven on earth?"

"Sorry," he said, smirking. "A guy has to have some secrets." As soon as the word *secrets* left his mouth, he grimaced, desperately wanting to swallow it back down. She did not need a reminder of the fact that he'd been keeping vital details of his life from her.

Zya opened her mouth to say something, no doubt something to put him in his place about his secrets, but then she snapped her mouth shut and just shook her head. After another bite, she pointed her fork at him and said, "I'll get that ingredient out of you sooner or later. You mark my words."

Grateful that she'd sidestepped their awkward moment, he put his fork down and shook his head. "Sorry to be the bearer of bad news, but that's one that stays in the family." He glanced at Winnie. "One day the secret will be hers."

Sighing dramatically, Zya put her fork down and crossed her arms over her chest. "That's just mean, Brody. You know that's one thing you could say to get me to give up on the ingredient hunt, right?"

He grinned at her. "Sorry, Zy. You'll just have to find something else to needle me about."

"I'm sure I'll find something." She ate the last of her pancakes and then turned her attention to Winnie, who was half covered in jam and whipped cream. Chuckling, she said, "Come on, Winnie. Let's get you cleaned up."

"Oh, no," Brody said, quickly standing. "I can't let you do that. I'll take her—"

"You can, and you will," Zya said firmly. "You clean up the kitchen. Winnie and I will be back in a few minutes."

Brody watched as his two favorite girls left the kitchen, and he had a sudden sense that maybe, just maybe, everything was finally going to be okay.

CHAPTER 3

Zya? Earth to Zya, a female voice called as the person waved her hand in front of Zya's face. *Are you in there?*

Zya blinked and focused on her great-aunt Helen floating on the other side of the counter next to the display of a new batch of her favorite alpaca yarn. Her *dead* great-aunt Helen. Just one of her many ancestors who liked to show up when she had her guards down. It happened more frequently when she was working in her store, Witches in Stitches, so she shouldn't be surprised that Helen was here now when she'd been deep in thought about her morning with Brody and Winnie. Stifling a sigh, knowing there was no getting rid of her anytime soon, Zya said, "Yes, I'm here."

"I can see that," a man said with a deep chuckle, startling her. "It appears I interrupted something important if you were that deep in your thoughts."

Holy hell. Where had he come from? Zya took in the tall older gentleman. He was wearing jeans and a Henley thermal that fit snug against his frame. He had wide shoulders, a narrow waist, and his exposed forearms were tanned and toned as if he spent his days working outside. He was the very definition of a silver fox.

He's gorgeous, right? Her aunt Helen said, fanning herself as if a ghost could suffer a hot flash.

Zya ignored her aunt and gave the gentleman a welcoming smile. "I'm sorry. You caught me daydreaming, it appears. What can I help you with? Are you looking for something in particular?"

"Yes, I am. But I think I've already found it." He leaned his hip against her front counter and eyed her with interest. "I met your aunt the other day, and she mentioned that you are relatively new to Keating Hollow and might be interested in meeting some new people."

Dread swept over Zya, knowing what was coming. "Aunt Helen?"

"Yes. She's a lovely woman, and if she weren't a ghost, I'd have asked her out in a heartbeat."

Zya cast a glare at her aunt, who only smiled innocently. Then she turned her attention back to the man and cleared her throat. "So, Mister…"

He held out his hand. "Charles Allen. I own a lumber mill just outside of Keating Hollow."

She took his hand in hers. "It's nice to meet you, Charles. I guess you already know my name."

"Zya Rossi. You own this yarn shop and have the gift of speaking to spirits."

Gift. Sure, if that's what one wanted to call it. If you asked her, it was more like a burden. If she didn't do the work to keep them away from her home, she'd be inundated twenty-four-seven with spirits who just wanted to be heard. Or ones like her Aunt Helen or Aunt Vera, both of whom were determined to get her married off to someone of means.

"I assume this means you can also speak to spirits if you've had a conversation with my aunt," Zya said, trying to remain polite while she figured out how to exit this conversation.

"Sort of." He shrugged slightly. "They come to me in my dreams. I've never really seen or heard them while I was awake."

"You dreamwalked him?" Zya blurted the accusation at her aunt, who was still floating near Charles. "You know you're not supposed to do that."

Her aunt didn't even bother to look sheepish. *He was open to it. What's the big deal?*

"Is Helen here?" Charles asked, looking around the store, trying to spot her.

"She's right next to you," Zya said.

A slow grin spread across his lips as he stared past her aunt. "Hello again."

Her aunt's cheeks turned pink as she flushed. Yes, a ghost can flush, even if they are no-longer in their flesh-and-bone body. Their bodies are just a manifestation of who they used to be, so blushing is no different than anything else they manifest.

"She's pleased to see you again, too," Zya said dryly, coming to the conclusion that they were a perfect match, despite what must have been a fifty plus year age difference.

Charles must have caught on to Zya's impatience because he turned his attention back to her and said, "Listen, I know we just met, but I'd really like to take you out and show you around the area."

"I—"

The only person you've been out with lately is Brinn, her aunt said.

"Yes, but—" She'd started to say that now that Brody was in town, that would change, but before she could get the words out, Charles cut her off.

"No buts!" Charles beamed at her. "I've already got the day planned. Helen said you have Sundays off, so I thought we'd go to a car show and then there's a gathering over at the Pelsh winery in the afternoon. We'll make a day of it."

Zya frowned, trying to come up with a way to let the man down easy.

"Here." He placed a card on her counter and said, "I have to run. Meet me at Incantation Café at ten on Sunday, and I'll get you a coffee before we go."

"That's—"

The doorbell chimed and the man was gone before she could even finish her sentence.

"Helen!" Zya cried, staring at her aunt. "You coached him, didn't you?"

Her aunt widened her eyes. *I have no idea what you're talking about.*

"Liar." Zya shook her head in disgust. "I should just not show up."

You will, and we both know it, Helen said, grinning from ear to ear. *But I don't know why you wouldn't want to. The man is gorgeous, accomplished, and very sweet. You could do a lot worse. Like that Brody character. You haven't heard from him in months, and now he's in your house, eating your food, and expecting you to help raise his daughter. You deserve so much better, Zya.*

Zya clenched her fists, refusing to engage in this conversation. All of her relatives, both dead and alive, had a thing against Brody. A thing that was irrational. They didn't seem to understand a man and a woman being just friends. And when Brody was around, they thought… Well, she wasn't sure what they thought. That he was stringing her along? Using her? Making it harder for her to date because her best friend was a man? Zya wasn't sure what their problem was, but she'd made a point of not making it her problem. Brody was her person. No one ever said someone's person couldn't be someone who was just a friend.

I wouldn't be surprised to learn that Carter left you because of your relationship with Brody, Helen said with a sniff.

"That's it. Out!" Zya pointed to the front door as if her aunt would ever actually leave a building that way. "Neither you nor anyone else is going to blame me for that fiasco of a relationship. He was cheating on me, with multiple women. Nothing I did deserved that kind of treatment, and I will not tolerate your insinuations."

Her aunt's complexion turned white. *That's not… I just meant that Brody's the only one you really open up to about things, and that makes it hard to have a romantic relationship when your partner feels like someone else is more important.*

"Go," Zya said flatly. She'd had this argument with her aunts before. They firmly believed that Zya would never find someone as long as she had Brody in her life. She wasn't going to sacrifice her best friend just to please some insecure man.

A small voice in the back of her head argued that while her aunts were out of line, there was a kernel of truth there. She'd always loved Brody as more than a friend and as long as that was the case, she wasn't sure she could give her heart fully to someone else.

That still didn't mean that Carter wasn't a grade-A jackass.

He was to blame for their broken engagement. One hundred percent.

Carter knew you didn't want to marry him, Helen said, her voice holding firm. *Knowing the woman you love doesn't love you back is devastating for a man.*

It appeared that since Zya couldn't banish her aunt, Helen was going to have her say no matter what Zya thought about it. Or how angry she got. "I am well aware of your feelings, Helen. You're wasting your time here. Brody is family. That's not going to change, no matter how much you badger me. You got what you came for, now let me get back to work."

You mean back to daydreaming about a ready-made family, she said just before she popped out of existence.

Zya clutched the counter, wanting to scream at her aunt, but it was no use. She was gone now and wouldn't be back for a long while if Zya could help it.

She only says those things because she worries about you, a soft voice said from behind her.

Son of a... Zya steeled herself and turned to look at her Aunt Vera. While Helen was tall and thin with long white hair, Vera was shorter and curvier with salt and lavender hair. She had just as many wrinkles as her sister, but she thought of herself as hip and wore all the latest fashions while Helen wore long, lacy black dresses, fully embracing the look of a witchy woman. "I guess I should have put up my protection spells as soon as Helen left."

Oh, come on now, Vera said gently. *I'm not here to berate you. I just thought you might need an ear to listen.*

Vera wasn't fooling Zya. They were playing good cop, bad cop. Admittedly, Vera was the more patient of the two, but they'd conspired for this to happen, and Helen no doubt had Vera's full support when she brought Charles to Zya's shop and then gave her an earful about how she'd never be happy until she pushed Brody away. "I'm fine. Thank you. Right now I have work to do."

Vera glanced around the empty shop. *I can see that,* she said dryly.

Zya rolled her eyes. "You know there is more work than just waiting on customers. I need to do inventory to place an order. So unless you want to count skeins of yarn, then I'd recommend we visit some other time."

You know inventory isn't my thing. Vera floated to hover next to Zya and then leaned in, brushing a kiss onto Zya's cheek. It wasn't a real kiss, more like a slight tickle, but Zya felt it all the same. *Just remember that we love you and if you need help with anything, we're here.*

"Sure," Zya said with a nod, but she knew she'd never call on them unless it was a true emergency. Her aunts' brand of help always errored on the unethical side. Like the time they slipped Kelly Winters a sleeping pill so that she missed prom and the boy who was supposed to take her was suddenly free to spend the evening with Zya. Talk about angry. Zya hadn't spoken to them for months.

Her aunts hadn't seen the problem. Kelly Winters had been the type to not care about anyone but herself. Selfish didn't even cover it. Opportunist was closer. They just saw it as giving her a dose of her own medicine. But that wasn't Zya's way. She wouldn't compromise her own morals just because someone else was a jerk. She had to live with herself after all.

It was Vera's turn to sigh. *One day you'll realize you don't have to do everything the hard way, dear. What's the point in being a witch if you never use your gifts?*

"I use them," Zya said, almost to herself. She just didn't use them in the ways that her aunts wanted her to.

Vera snorted. *Yeah, to keep us away.*

And to communicate with her wolf, but she didn't tell Vera that. She and Helen would only worry more. Who wanted to date a woman who could command a wolf? Talk about trust issues.

"If you'd stop trying to meddle in my life, I wouldn't have to shut you out," Zya said as sweetly as possible.

Everyone needs guidance every once in a while, Vera said.

"Even great-aunts who don't have anything better to do than to obsess over my love life."

We aren't obsessed. Just concerned.

"Well, don't be. I'm perfectly fine." Zya grabbed her tablet and moved to the back of the store to start her inventory.

A moment later, she heard the chime on the door and prayed that meant Vera had left, though she knew that was wishful thinking. Vera popped in and out just like Helen did.

"Zya?" a familiar female voice called. "Are you here?"

"Brinn?" Zya poked her head out from behind a rack and smiled at her friend.

"Do you know there is a ghost in your store?" Brinn asked, eyeing Vera who was now sitting in an arm chair as if she were waiting for Zya to finish so that they could resume their conversation.

Oh, a live one, Vera said, her eyes flashing with mischief. *It's so exciting when we find out someone else can see us lurking around town.*

"You've done it now. Brinn, this is my great-aunt Vera. Vera, this is Brinn, my friend," Zya said, casting a sidelong glance at her aunt. "Please leave Brinn alone. She has enough issues with spirits following her around."

Vera held her hands up in a surrender motion. *I have no*

plans to harass your friend. Not unless she has a cute brother who doesn't mind being dreamwalked.

"Uh…" Brinn started.

"Just don't say anything," Zya warned her. "Engaging will only encourage her."

"Okay," Brinn said, glancing around, looking slightly uncomfortable.

Who could blame her? Six years ago, Brinn had moved back to Keating Hollow just to get away from seeing ghosts all the time. That had worked for a while, but now she was seeing them again. Zya had taken her under her wing to teach her how to put up walls so that ghosts couldn't bother her all the time, and now here was Vera, just hanging out as if ghosts were completely normal. To Zya, they were, but she understood Brinn's feelings. No one wanted to feel like they were being watched by random ghosts all the time.

"Vera was just going," Zya said, giving her aunt a warning glare.

No, I'm not. Not yet anyway, Vera said. *We still have things to talk about.*

Zya let out a low groan of irritation. "This is what I get for running out of time this morning," she told Brinn. "I was in a hurry and didn't strengthen my shields."

"I didn't either, but that's probably because I haven't seen a ghost in a while," Brinn said with a grimace. "I've gotten lazy."

"What do you say we do that now?" Zya asked her friend as she gave her aunt a smirk.

Okay, fine. Vera lifted her arms in defeat and stood from her chair. *I'll go before the two of you send me somewhere hellish. But I'm not happy about it.* Vera glanced at Brinn. *Do me a favor, will you?*

Brinn raised both eyebrows, waiting to see what Vera might say.

Make sure she goes out with someone other than Brody Saxon. The only thing that lies with that boy is heartbreak.

Zya clenched her jaw and forced herself to not lash out at Vera. Though her aunt deserved it. How dare they keep trying to control her life? She was thirty-two years old. She didn't need two great-aunts who came of age in the 1950s to tell her how to run her life. But arguing would only prolong the ghost's departure.

"Well, that's easy," Brinn said, grinning. "That's why I'm here."

"What?" Zya cried. "Oh my goddess, Aunt Helen got to you, didn't she?"

"Who?" Brinn asked, looking over at Vera.

My sister. Zya thinks she coerced you into coming here to set her up on a date. Vera eyed Brinn curiously. *Did she?*

Brinn cleared her throat. "No. I've never met Helen." She lowered her voice and, in a barely audible whisper, added, "Thank the goddess."

Zya felt the tension drain from her shoulders. But then she remembered that Brinn was trying to set her up, and a ball of anxiety formed in her chest, making her rub at her breast plate. "I'm not really interested in dating," she told her friend.

Brinn gave her a sympathetic look.

She was the one person in Keating Hollow whom she'd told about Carter. Her friend knew that Zya was still raw over the entire thing. That's why it surprised Zya that Brinn wanted to set her up with someone.

"It's not like that," Brinn said, shaking her head. "It's not a blind date... exactly. I mean, it kinda is, but it's dinner with me and Austin and a friend of his who is visiting from out of town.

So a foursome with no expectations of you seeing each other again. He's a musician, so it's not like he's staying in Keating Hollow," she said, rambling a bit. "He's a guitar player between gigs, and he's working with Austin on a new project. You know how it is. They get holed up in the studio and don't see people for days. I figured this would be a nice break."

A musician. Zya never could say no to the ones in a band, Vera said with a gleam in her eye. *Thank you, Brinn. I'm pretty sure you just found her weakness.* Vera waved her fingers at both of them and then, cackling like a loon, she vanished into thin air.

"She was… a lot," Brinn said carefully.

"That she is. Sorry about that." Zya held her hands out to Brinn and wasn't surprised when Brinn took them without question. Together they chanted the spell that would strengthen their shields to keep the spirits from showing themselves to them.

It wasn't that spirits were evil or even bad. It was just overwhelming and a huge invasion on a medium's life. Imagine being one of the very few people who could see and speak to spirits. When there were ghosts who had something to say, it was a huge imposition on the witch who had to endure them until they felt their issue was dealt with properly. Sometimes that was five minutes; other times it was five years.

No one deserved that kind of never-ending intrusion.

Magic crackled around the two women. It would've been stronger if Zya had access to water, but combining their strength would do a decent enough job of keeping her relatives away for at least a few days. As the magic skittered across her skin, feeling like more of a whisper than a command, she mentally made a note to get Brinn out to the lagoon so they could improve the spell sometime, sooner rather than later.

Together they called out, *"Protegere!"*

A flash of white surrounded them like a silo and then slowly dissipated, indicating that the spell had worked.

"I'm not sure I'll ever really get used to that," Brinn said, wiping the beads of sweat from her brow.

"I haven't," Zya admitted. "Not really. There's not anything normal about magic pouring from one's fingertips. If it was, everyone could do it."

There were plenty of witches in Keating Hollow who could wield magic, but the truth was, most of them weren't as strong as Zya and used their magic in other ways. Like Brody did when he was cultivating his grape vines. It was a subtle, nuanced magic, while Zya's was erratic at best and wild at worst. She could make things happen with her magic, but only because she did it by brute force. She would not be the witch anyone would call if they needed a delicate touch.

"Thank you," Brinn said. "Now, about that dinner…"

Zya laughed. "Fine, I'll go to dinner with you, Austin, and the guitar player. Happy? Where should I meet you after I close the store?"

Brinn rattled off the information, hugged her, and hurried off, saying something about needing to run a few errands.

Just as Brinn left, Zya's phone rang. Her entire body sagged in relief when she saw Brody's name flash across the screen. "Hey, you. What's up?"

"I just need to know which your cat prefers, tuna or salmon?"

"You're feeding my cat fresh fish?" Zya asked, confused.

"No," he said with a chuckle. "I'm at the store, trying to restock your cupboards, and I saw Lyra's food brand. It's on sale. I just wondered which is her favorite."

"Secret option number three," Zya said, feeling a warmth in her belly. He'd remembered to even get food for Lyra. There was just no way around it; he was a keeper. "Chicken is her favorite, followed by salmon."

"Got it. Need anything else while I'm at the store?" he asked.

It was on the tip of her tongue to say, *you*. But she shook herself and went with the safe bet. "Ice cream. Chocolate caramel swirl."

Brody chuckled. "Some things really never change, do they?"

"Not when it comes to chocolate caramel swirl," she agreed.

"I should've known. See you around six?"

Her nerves fluttered as she tried to figure out the best way to tell him she wouldn't be there.

"Zy? Will you be here for dinner?" he asked.

"No?" The word came out sounding more like a question than a statement.

He chuckled. "You sound unsure."

"I'm not." She shook her head even though he couldn't see her and added, "I have dinner plans with Brinn. I'm not sure when I'll be home." It wasn't a total lie, right? She was having dinner with her friend. She just hadn't wanted to mention a blind date. He'd make a thing of it, teasing and giving her "the talk" like he always did when she said she had a date. Tonight she just wanted to do Brinn this favor and then go home and find out if Brody had found a place.

The thought hit her like a ton of bricks. She absolutely did not want Brody and Winnie to leave her house. It had only been one night with one breakfast, and Zya already wanted that life... with him.

She knew it wasn't healthy. She also knew that her aunts might have a point about her being unable to move forward while she had feelings for Brody. But she still didn't forgive them their meddling.

"Okay," Brody said cheerfully. "I'll see you when you get in, and we'll chat over ice cream."

"Sounds perfect." After Zya ended the call, she glanced at the wall clock and mentally started to count down the hours until she could be curled up on her couch with a pint of ice cream in one hand and an Irish cream coffee in the other.

CHAPTER 4

*B*rody followed his realtor, Wanda Danvers, into the Mystyk Pizza Parlor. After he'd run to the store, he'd spent the better part of the afternoon looking for a place to live. Any place. It had not been fruitful. As it turned out, there just weren't many places to rent or even buy in Keating Hollow. In fact, there were two options. One was a studio apartment above a garage, and the other was a broken-down ranch on just over six acres outside of town, which would be great if it were just Brody.

Starting his own hobby vineyard had always been a dream of Brody's. Not one that would be large enough to be in competition with his employer, but one where he could hone is craft and maybe sell to a few of the local establishments.

The problem was that the house just wasn't habitable at the moment. He wasn't afraid of putting in some work on a place, but having a three-year-old in a construction zone was an absolute no. The ranch-style house needed to be gutted and reroofed, not to mention the barn that was caving in on itself. The property was beautiful, and he was seriously considering purchasing it, but they couldn't live there until the majority of the work was done.

"That ranch is just perfect for you," Wanda said, beaming at him as they waited for the hostess to seat them. "I saw the way you looked when you walked the property. I always know when my clients have found the right place."

"I do love it," he admitted. "I was just hoping for something a little more—"

"Livable?" Wanda finished for him.

He chuckled. "Exactly. It's a lot of work and I have my daughter…"

"I understand completely," Wanda said. "My partner and I built our own place. It took a lot, but in the end, it's been worth it. Only you can answer the question of whether it's worth it to you."

He nodded and followed as they were led to a table in the back of the restaurant. As they took their seats, he fumbled with his menu and asked, "Are you sure Blake is okay with watching Winnie? I don't want to take advantage."

"Trust me, she wouldn't have offered if she didn't want to," Wanda said. "She's been saving up for a car, so the extra money is motivating. Don't worry. Blake is really good with kids. She's a spirit witch and can read their energy, so she isn't caught off guard when someone has a meltdown or needs a nap or even when they need a hug. I keep telling her she should do something to work with kids, but so far she hasn't chosen anything specific."

"I thought she said she's in college," Brody said, wondering if he should've asked more questions before leaving his daughter with a stranger. Granted, Blake was Wanda's sister, so it wasn't like he'd just found someone off the street, but when

Winnie started to have a meltdown because she needed a nap, Blake had offered to babysit and Brody had been so grateful, he'd just taken her up on it. He needed to find a place to live and the sooner the better. He couldn't keep imposing on Zya.

"That's right," Wanda said. "Right now she's taking online college classes and doing call center work from her computer, but she hates the call center job. As soon as she finds something else, she'll give them notice."

"Sounds like she's a responsible young lady," Brody said.

Wanda chuckled. "Don't worry, Dad. Your girl is in good hands. Besides, Cameron is home. If there's an emergency, he's right there to help."

"That does make me feel better," Brody said, feeling slightly ridiculous. People left their kids with babysitters all the time. As much as he didn't want to leave her with someone else, he wasn't sure there was any other choice. There was no getting around it; he'd need help raising his daughter. That probably meant another nanny, but he wasn't looking forward to hiring one. The one that had worked for him briefly in France had been far too severe for his liking.

It wasn't long before a waiter stopped by their table and took their order. Once he left, Brody excused himself to use the restroom. On his way back, he did a double-take when he spotted Zya squeezed into a booth with a large man who had his arm draped across her shoulders.

He blinked, taking in the scene. Another couple was sitting across from them. The blonde, a pretty woman wearing a lace-up top, was telling a story and waving her hands animatedly. Everyone was focused on her except Zya. Her gaze had met Brody's. She widened her eyes as if giving him some sort of signal and then mouthed, *help.*

31

Without another thought, he hurried over to the booth with a bright smile. "Hey, Zya. Fancy meeting you here."

She gave him a tight smile and said, "Yeah, well, a girl has to eat, right?"

"Sure," he said with a nod, wondering when she'd made plans. She hadn't said anything about a date earlier, just that she was meeting her friend Brinn for dinner. Not that she owed him any sort of explanation when it came to where she went and when. He was just a guest in her house after all. Well, not *just* a guest. He was her friend. But that didn't mean she needed to check in with him every time she went out. He glanced around at the small group and said, "Hi. I'm Brody. Zya's best friend."

"Oh, hi!" the blonde said as she held her hand out to him. "I'm Brinn and this is my fiancé, Austin." She pointed to the dark-haired man, who waved at Brody. Brinn turned her attention to Zya's date and added, "And this is—"

"Kayce Perry," Brody finished for her the moment he really looked at Zya's date. "The lead guitarist for Midnight Rain."

The guitarist gave Brody a wide smile. "You're a fan, huh?"

"You might say that." Brody gave the guitarist a sheepish grin. "Your riff in "Stilettos" is one of the only ways I can get my three-year-old daughter to go to sleep some nights."

The man winced and playfully brought his fist to his heart and mimed stabbing himself in the chest. "Damn man, that was harsh. You're telling me my playing is so boring it puts your kid to sleep?"

"No, no!" Brody waved his hands, indicating that the man had taken his statement the wrong way. "Not at all. She just loves it so much that as soon as it comes on, she settles as she listens to it. It sort of calms her. I'm not sure why, but usually shortly after the song ends, her eyes grow heavy and she passes out. I'm not questioning it. As long as she gets to sleep, that's all I care about."

"Well, that might just be the nicest, though strangest, compliment I've ever gotten," Kayce said with a shake of his head. "Maybe I can come play it live for her sometime."

"That would be amazing," Brody said automatically, because he wasn't going to pass up the chance to hang with a member of one of the hottest rock bands in the country. Winnie might not appreciate it quite as much as he would, but she'd no doubt love the music.

Zya cleared her throat. "Where is Winnie right now?"

Brody turned his attention to his friend, who looked slightly annoyed. "She's with Wanda's sister. We went looking for houses so that we can get out of your spare bedrooms."

A troubled expression flashed on her pretty face for just a second before her neutral mask slid into place. "Did you find one?"

"I think so, but I'm just not sure yet if it will work out." He shoved his hands in his pockets. "It's a property just outside of town on six acres, but it needs a lot of work."

"The old Vincent place?" Brinn asked.

He nodded. He was pretty sure that's what Wanda had called it.

"It is a beautiful piece of property," Brinn said. "But you're right. It needs a lot of work."

Zya glanced past him, her eyes focusing on something. He turned to find Wanda standing behind him.

"I'm sorry to interrupt," Wanda said with a pleasant smile. "Brody, I just got word that there's another offer coming in on the Vincent place. I don't want to pressure you at all, but if you're really serious about it, you're going to need to get your offer in as soon as possible."

"Right after Brody looked at it?" Zya asked incredulously. "Seems a little suspicious, don't you think?"

"No. Not really. Not in this market. The property has only been on the MLS for two days. Considering the growth that Keating Hollow has seen the past few years, I'd really expect a property with that much usable land to sell quickly."

"Can we go back out and see it again?" Brody asked. "Tonight?"

"I'm sure it isn't a problem since no one is living there, but let me just contact the listing agent." She stepped away and pressed the phone to her ear.

"Are you really that serious about the property?" Zya asked.

Brody nodded slowly. "I think I might be."

Zya frowned and opened her mouth to say something, but Wanda appeared beside Brody again and said, "We're all set. Do you want to go now or after we eat?"

He glanced at the table where their pizza had just arrived. "Can we take the pizza to go? I don't want to lose what's left of the daylight."

"Absolutely." Wanda hurried across the restaurant to talk to the waiter.

Brody met Zya's eyes and said, "I better go. I'll—"

"Not without me," Zya said, gesturing to her date to let her out of the booth. "Sorry, Kayce. But I can't let my best friend make this kind of decision without a second opinion."

Kayce looked startled but slid out of the booth, letting her go.

Zya looked at Brinn and gave her an apologetic smile. "Sorry. But you understand, right?"

"Of course," Brinn said. "Go on. I'll talk to you later."

Zya held her hand out to the guitarist. "It was really nice

meeting you. I hope you enjoy your stay here in Keating Hollow."

Kayce cut his gaze to Brody and then back to Zya as he held her hand for a beat too long.

Brody wanted to tug his best friend away from the guy, but kept himself in check. He had no business manhandling her… no matter how much he wanted to. He clenched his jaw and waited for her to extract herself from the musician. Maybe he didn't want to spent an afternoon with the rocker after all. Not when all he could think about was how much he wanted to deck the man for just holding Zya's hand.

"Would you mind if I ask Brinn for your number?" Kayce asked her.

"Uh…" she started.

"You know, so I can come play for Brody's little girl," he added.

"Oh, right. Sure." She gave him an authentic smile this time.

Brody didn't like it. He was under no illusions. He knew Kayce was asking for her number just so that he could see her again. Zya just had an air about her that attracted men. Even when she seemed uninterested. Or maybe they were even more determined to win her over when she didn't give them the time of day. He'd seen it over and over and over again.

"We're set," Wanda said, appearing beside him with a pizza box. "Ready?"

"Yes." Brody placed his hand on the small of Zya's back and added, "Zya's coming along. I hope that's okay."

"Of course it is." Wanda smiled at Zya. "I can't wait for you to see this place. I think you'll agree that it's perfect."

Once they were in Wanda's car, Wanda glanced back at Zya, who was in the back seat. "Kayce Perry, huh? What did you think of him? Cool guy or typical ego-ridden rock star?"

"He was… fine," she said with a half shrug.

Brody narrowed his eyes at her. "What exactly did he do to make him just *fine*?" It wasn't a word she used often. Zya was usually much more expressive.

She let out a soft chuckle. "He was polite, even charming at times. But you know how I feel about overly touchy-feely people. He kept putting his hand on my knee, and all I wanted to do was knee him in the groin."

"You should have," Brody muttered. "Who does he think he is, getting handsy with a woman he just met?"

Wanda cackled. "He thinks he's Kayce Perry, the gifted guitarist from Midnight Rain. I'm sure he's used to plenty of women who are dying for him to touch them."

"Not this one," Zya said, knowing she sounded like a prude. But the date hadn't been her idea, and although she appreciated the artistry of what Kayce did, that didn't mean she was ready to jump into bed with him. She never had been one for jumping into bed with someone right away. She was the type who needed to get to know someone first. "Besides, did you see that beauty mark over his left eye?"

Brody felt his lips twitch in amusement.

"I did," Wanda said with a solemn nod. "It's unfortunate, isn't it? The sign of a life cursed to endure bad luck. Though I'd say with his success, maybe he's dodged that particular bullet."

"I'm not willing to hang around and find out," Zya said. "Been there, done that before. Nope. Not messing with anyone who has the left eye beauty mark."

Brody eyed his raven-haired friend and then said, "Starting tomorrow, I'm drawing one on my face. Right here." He pressed his forefinger to his flesh just above his left eye. "You know, just to test that theory."

Zya rolled her eyes. "Sure, Brody. When you figure out how to use the beauty pencil, then I'll start worrying about it."

"I know what I'm doing. I watch *Drag Race*," he said with a sniff.

With her eyebrows raised in surprise, Zya said, "Since when?"

"Since I worked with a girl whose brother was on the show," he said. "She had a viewing party. Turns out, it's entertaining as hell." He winked at her. "You should give it a try."

"Oh, it's fabulous," Wanda said. "Those girls really know how to turn it out." She sighed. "If only I'd been a man, then I could've won that show. Mark my words, I'd have been the best drag queen this side of the Atlantic Ocean."

Zya met Brody's gaze and the pair of them cackled.

"No doubt, Wanda," Zya said. "No doubt."

CHAPTER 5

*Z*ya walked the fence line of the old Vincent property, her heart heavy. The moment they'd turned into the long drive that led up to the house, she'd known this was Brody's place. She could just feel it in her bones. But why did that make her so sad?

She should be ecstatic that her best friend was talking about putting down roots in Keating Hollow. When she'd moved to the small magical town just over a year ago, she'd never dreamed that Brody would end up just a few miles away. She was happy that he was here, right? Then why was the possibility of him moving across town bumming her out?

Because you want him to stay at your house, the voice in the back of her mind said.

Zya let out a little groan and shook herself. She had to stop this nonsense.

Of course Brody was going to move out and find his own place. Why wouldn't he? It's not like they'd ever lived together before. Not really. There were a few times when they'd used each other's couches for a couple of weeks when they were between relationships. But there was never any discussion of them sharing space for a significant amount of time.

That wasn't something Zya could do anyway. If she had to witness him dating...

Oh, hell, she thought. That was it, wasn't it? Now that he had Winnie, she hadn't expected him to bring women home and if that was the case, she just wanted him around.

Damn. Blowing out a long breath, Zya shook off all her intrusive thoughts and really looked around at the property. The rolling hills gave way to a gorgeous view of the mountains. The sky was pink with the fading sunset, the color bouncing off the white peaks.

"Just lovely," she whispered, imagining rows and rows of grapes on the horizon.

The land was already cleared, and there appeared to be some sort of irrigation system already in place. Surely it would need work like the barn and the house, but having the structure there would be very useful.

The barn needed to be completely redone, and the house looked like a gut job. She didn't know how much work Brody wanted to put into it, but the land... That was what made the place so special.

"Did you see the river?" Brody asked, joining her on her path along the dilapidated fence.

"No. Where is it?" she asked even as she opened her senses and started walking toward the east.

Brody chuckled and fell into step beside her. "I knew you'd find it as soon as I mentioned it."

Zya was a spirit witch with an affinity for water. It was where she felt the most powerful, and if she opened herself to it, she could always find it easily. "The property is perfect for a small winery."

"It really is," he agreed. "But is it perfect for me?"

"Only you can answer that, Brody. How much work do you want to do? The house is salvageable, but not livable for a while. And the barn—"

"It's a total loss, I know," he said.

"Looks like you need to ask yourself if you have the funds to start a business *and* rehab the house."

"I do if I do a bunch of the remodeling myself," he said.

Zya came to a stop at the top of a bluff and looked down at the churning river below. The landscape nearly took her breath away. Magical energy filled her up from the inside out and if she'd had her way, she'd be the one buying the property. It didn't matter that she'd have to spend the next ten years making it livable. That spot made it all worth it.

She turned to Brody and took both of his hands in hers. The moment they touched, a spark of magic skittered across their skin. "Feel that?"

His eyes were wide and full of wonder. "Is that coming from this land?"

She nodded. "It's a magical place, Brody. One filled with so much hope and possibility. You'd be a fool if you don't snatch it up."

Brody held her gaze for a long moment and then nodded. "I think you're right." Then he frowned and grimaced as he said, "I guess this means I'm also leasing that studio apartment, then."

She frowned at him. "What? Why?"

"Winnie and I need somewhere to live, and I don't want to be running back and forth from Eureka to Keating Hollow every day."

Zya tsked and gave her friend a look of disgust. "Is there something wrong with my house?"

He blinked at her. "No. Of course not. But you don't want me and Winnie staying at your house for months. I can't ask that of you."

"Well you sure as hell can't live in a studio apartment for months with a three-year-old either. No. You will not rent that place. You will stay with me in my three-bedroom house for as long as you need." She swept her arm out, indicating the house behind them. "Until this place is done so you're not devoting part of your resources to rent. Understand?"

"Zya, I can't—"

"Nope. I will not take no for an answer. You will stay with me for as long as it takes, and I wouldn't have it any other way. If it doesn't work out for either of us, we'll just be honest and then you can start looking for another temporary place. But not a studio. At least a two bedroom. What do you say?"

Brody's lips twitched up into an amused smile. "You're not going to let me say no, are you?"

"What gave it away?" she asked with her hands on her hips as she pinned him with her stare.

Shaking his head, he wrapped his arms around her and pulled her into a tight hug. "You're the best, Zya. Thank you."

Zya pressed her head against his firm chest and held on. "I know. You're okay, too."

His body shook with silent laughter as he kissed the top of her head. Then he let go far too soon and took a step back. "Should we go tell Wanda to get the paperwork started?"

"Definitely." Together, they walked back up to the main driveway where they found Wanda leaning against her SUV.

"That grin on your face makes me think you've made a decision," Wanda said.

"I have." Brody gestured for her to follow him as he made

his way onto the shoddy-looking porch. "All we need to do now is talk numbers."

Zya turned and stared at the mountain off in the distance. It was amazing how after only living in Keating Hollow for a year, that she'd come to think of the place as home in a way that she never had in Salem. At first, she'd thought her feelings for Keating Hollow were just a result of needing to get away from her past. From Carter, her cheating ex, and her family who always had expectations of her that she could never seem to fill. In their eyes, she was supposed to be married by now with two kids and a dog while working in the family herb shop where her mother and living aunts could try to dictate her life. At least now all she had to deal with were her dead aunts trying to fix her up with anyone they deemed a suitable husband.

A small shiver ran down her spine.

The idea of getting married had always made her slightly uneasy. Now that she had a broken engagement behind her, it was a thousand times worse. Where would she be now if she'd married Carter and then found out about his extracurricular activities? Likely she'd be in the middle of a nasty divorce and broke as hell after fighting settlement demands and paying for lawyers. Her entire body went cold as she realized that had almost been her.

It was enough to make a girl swear off marriage forever. What did she need a ring for? She had her house, her shop, and a loyal wolf who accompanied her on her morning walks. She didn't need a man coming in and messing up her carefully curated life.

Or one who was so jealous that she had a male best friend that he acted like he was entitled to an affair or two on the side. Like Carter.

The jackass.

"Ready?" Brody asked when he joined her by Wanda's SUV.

"Only if you are," she said, giving him a soft smile. She really was happy for him. This property had the potential to make all his dreams come true.

"I am. Let's get Winnie and go home."

"Home," she said with a nod as warmth spread through her chest and a pleased smile claimed her lips. For now at least, they were claiming the same space as home. It was all she'd ever really wanted.

CHAPTER 6

"No, Mom," Brody said, unable to hide the impatience in this tone. "We are not coming back to Salem. My job is here and Winnie starts school this week."

"Why are you doing this to us, Brody?" she asked in a halted tone as she sniffled. "We've already lost so much time with Winnie. I can't believe you just left without saying a word. What have I done to deserve this?"

"I'm not doing anything to *you*, Mom," Brody said, kicking himself for answering the call at all. He had been expecting a call from Wanda about the house he'd offered on, and because he'd been busy making dinner, he hadn't paid attention to the caller ID. "I'm just trying to make the best life I can for me and my daughter."

"Away from your family? Away from her grandmother and grandfather?" she asked incredulously. "How is that best for anyone?"

Brody was tempted to just end the call. This was not a fight he could win with his mother. Nothing he said would get her to understand that he'd needed to get away from them. From

Salem. From the life they'd cultivated that he'd hated since he was a child. "I can't help it that my job is on the West Coast, mother. This just isn't about you. You get that, right?"

"It sure feels like it's about me. First you ran off to France and now California. You know, your father and I were perfectly willing to help you with Winnie. She needs family right now. Who is going to take care of her while you're working?"

"She'll be in preschool, and when she's not, a nanny will care for her. That's exactly what would happen if we'd stayed in Salem. The only difference is I'd be working for Dad instead of in my chosen career," he said, his jaw tight with tension. Why was he having to justify his choices to his mother, the woman who'd never spent a day in her life looking after him as a child. He'd had three different nannies so that there was never a time when his parents had to be inconvenienced to take care of him.

"No one said you had to work for your father," she said, her tone cold. "Although I don't know why you wouldn't want to. VP of his company, stock options, access to a private plane. It's an opportunity most young men would kill for."

"No doubt." He'd had this conversation at least a dozen times over the past few years. Stephen Saxon wanted his son to come work for him so that he could be groomed to take over the company someday. The problem was that Brody had never had one iota of interest in the high finance sector. He was an earth witch who was extremely talented at winemaking. All he wanted to do was cultivate the best grapes possible and make award-winning wines. There wasn't any place else on earth that made him happier than a vineyard or a wine cellar. "It's just not my passion, Mother. You know that."

"You always were so stubborn," she spit out. "I don't know

why you couldn't be like Theodore Woodsvale. He went to work for his father and has an art gallery on the side."

As if running a vineyard was even remotely like opening a gallery and then hiring a manager to run it. Still, that wasn't the point. "There's no point in discussing this. I'm not going to work for dad. I like my job, and Winnie and I are going to settle here in Keating Hollow. That's the end of the discussion."

"Well," she said with a huff of disapproval, "I was just trying to come up with some alternatives so that I wouldn't be cut off from my granddaughter permanently. You don't have to be rude about it."

He wanted to scream. "Why do you think you'll be cut off from Winnie permanently? It's not like I banned you from visiting."

"You just won't visit us, though. Right?" That coldness was back, and there was no sign of tears. He'd wondered if they were fake when he'd answered his phone.

"I don't have any plans for that soon. I'm just starting a new job, and Winnie is starting preschool. I just don't know what the immediate future looks like right now. Please tell me you understand."

"I understand that you want to keep me and your father away from Winnie. That's what I understand."

"Well, the truth is that right now, considering the way you're acting, there might be some truth to that," he snapped. "Do you think any of this has been easy on me? The last thing I need from you right now is a guilt trip. If you want to see Winnie, you can come visit. But don't plan on us making the trip back east in the near future. It's just not in the cards."

There was dead silence on the other end of the connection.

Brody waited, knowing that she hadn't hung up. Likely she

was fuming and weighing exactly how she was going to make him pay for his outburst.

Finally, in that steely voice of hers, she asked, "And where exactly are your father and I supposed to stay when we arrive in that tiny town of yours way out in the woods? In a cheap motel off the interstate forty miles away?"

He hung his head, hating that his parents were so effing pretentious. "No one would make you stay at a motel, Mom. There's a lovely inn here in town that I'm sure would be suitable, and there's also an upscale B&B. The town isn't *that* small."

"I see you didn't invite us to stay at your place. Don't most parents stay with their children when they come to visit?"

Not his parents. They'd never stayed with him. Not even when he'd had a posh apartment in Paris. They'd visited, sure. But they'd secured a suite at a five-star hotel. This was an obvious fishing-for-information question. He wasn't biting. "My place isn't ready yet, but when it is, you'll be the first to know. And when that happens, I'd be happy to make up the guest room for you."

"So you found a place already, then?"

"I think so. I'm working on it. Look, Mom, I have to go before I burn dinner. I'll talk to you later."

"Where are—"

He hit End and tossed the phone on the counter, knowing he'd never hear the end of hanging up on her. But he just couldn't deal with her a moment longer.

"Are you okay?" Zya asked softly from behind him.

Brody quickly spun around, startled by her presence, and then slumped against the counter. "Yeah, I'm fine."

"You don't look fine," she said, giving him a sympathetic smile.

He waved an impatient hand. "There's nothing I can do about my parents, so there's no sense in worrying about it. They're mad I left. What else is new? The only difference now compared to when I went to France is that they think my daughter is a weapon they can wield over me to get us to move back."

"I'm sorry." Zya stepped forward and wrapped her arms around Brody, hugging him.

He held her against him, grateful she was there holding him together. Of all the people in the world, she was his one friend who knew exactly what he was going through and would never question his decisions when it came to his parents. She knew exactly how toxic they could be and would support him unconditionally. He hadn't realized how much that mattered to him until Winnie became part of his life. "Thank you," he whispered.

"Always." She pressed her head into his chest like she always did and after a moment, with her arms encircling him, she glanced up. "Did you really invite them to Keating Hollow?"

He groaned and let his head fall back against one of the cupboards. "Don't remind me. I was just trying to diffuse her antics. I seriously doubt they'll show up here, though. Can you imagine my parents coming all the way here? My dad would blow a gasket when he realized the nearest Four Seasons is over two-hundred miles away."

"I don't know. Keating Hollow attracts a good amount of high-income people, especially from the entertainment industry. If they get wind of that, there's no telling what they might do."

"Seriously?" Brody asked, looking panicked. "How well known is that?"

"Not terribly," she said with a shrug. "Plus, Keating Hollow residents are good about protecting their own. They don't talk about the movie stars, directors, and musicians that call Keating Hollow home. But it's not a secret either."

"Son of a—"

"Daddy?" Winnie said in a sleepy voice.

Brody glanced over at the kitchen entrance and spotted his daughter holding PJ the dog and rubbing her sleepy eyes. "Hey, sweetheart."

He hurried over to her and scooped her up into his arms, hugging her too him. She wrapped her small arms around his neck and gave him a kiss on the cheek. His heart swelled so much he was certain it would burst right out of his chest.

Gaining her trust hadn't been easy in those first few weeks after her mother died. He'd spent many nights panicked about how he was going to raise a daughter on his own, but also heartbroken for her. Losing a mother at such a young age was devastating. But he was determined to make sure she knew she was loved and wanted. And after four weeks of being by her side every moment he could outside of work, she'd finally hugged him. Her tiny warm body had been plastered to his as if she was never going to let go, and it was in that moment that he'd completely fallen head over heels for her.

It was hard for him to even remember what life was like before she'd come to live with him. He'd fallen for her hard, and now he didn't even recognize the man who'd lived that carefree life with no commitments to anyone except himself. All he wanted to do was open his winery and settle in with his daughter… and Zya, too. He smiled at his friend and said, "Dinner's almost ready. Can you set the table?"

Zya, who was gazing at them with a tender expression, nodded. And when she turned, he could've sworn he'd seen a tear in her eye. But a few moments later, when she slipped past him, her eyes were clear and bright as she nudged him out of the way to get to the silverware drawer. "Well, are you going to finish this spaghetti dish, or am I going to have to do that, too?"

He rolled his eyes, put Winnie back down on her feet, and then walked back over to the stove where the sauce was simmering, and dumped the package of noodles into the boiling water. Then he got to work on the garlic bread. If it hadn't been for his mother's interruption, they'd already be sitting at the table.

Zya grabbed Winnie's hand and said, "Come on, girlfriend. We have a table to set."

As he waited for the noodles to cook, Brody leaned casually against the counter and grinned as he watched his best friend show his daughter how to set the table, one utensil at a time, before she ushered her outside so they could grab some greenery for the centerpiece.

By the time they were done, the dining room had a faint pine scent and was lit with three candles that made the place look magical. Just as it always did when Zya was around. Gods, he loved her.

The word *love* stopped him in his tracks. *Love.*

He *loved* Zya.

Of course he did; he'd always loved her. She was his best friend. But as he looked at her now, her face aglow from the candlelight as she whispered conspiratorially with his daughter, he couldn't deny that there was something more than just friendship between them.

He wanted her. Wanted Zya to be part of their lives. To share the winery he planned to open and to be more than just Winnie's aunt.

Brody quickly shook his head.

What was wrong with him? Here he was, after just two days at Zya's house, already losing his head over her. He'd thought he'd gotten a handle on that years ago.

Apparently not. And now it was worse, because he'd just committed to living with her for the foreseeable future.

Oh, hell.

"Brody?" Zya called.

He blinked. "Yeah?"

"The timer is going off."

The harsh sound of the oven timer finally penetrated his thick skull. "Right. Sorry, I was just…"

"Thinking about that phone call?" she asked.

No. Not even close. "Yeah. You know. Parents. Can't live with them—"

"Can't change your phone number," she joked.

He chuckled as he turned off the oven and pulled out the garlic bread.

When he set their plates on the table, Zya made a show of stuffing her napkin into her shirt so that it covered her entire chest. "This is how we eat spaghetti," Zya told Winnie. "That way we can slurp up those ends without worrying about where all the sauce goes." She took a bite, letting one of the noodles hang down and then sucking it into her mouth, making a loud obnoxious sound.

Winnie watched carefully and then fumbled as she stuffed her own napkin into her shirt.

Brody quickly fixed it for her, making sure the cloth napkin covered most of her body and then waiting for the inevitable mess that followed.

Winnie curled the spaghetti onto her fork like he'd shown her before and then stuffed way too much into her mouth, making Zya laugh when she tried unsuccessfully to slurp up the dangling ends.

"We'll work on it," Zya said as she wiped the sauce off Winnie's cheeks. When his daughter was mostly cleaned up, Zya held her fork over her plate. "Ready to try again?"

Winnie nodded and the two of them proceeded to slurp on their spaghetti. It was messy and chaotic, but Brody found himself wishing the night would never end.

CHAPTER 7

"Why am I doing this?" Zya asked herself as she parked her car a few spaces down from Incantation Café. It was Sunday, just before ten in the morning, and because she didn't want to be that person who stood anyone up, she was there for her date with Charles Allen. It was just one day, right? Surely she could spend a few hours, have lunch with the man, and then go on her way. Right?

"Right," she told herself and then hopped out of her Jeep and strolled into the café.

The tall man, who she guessed was in his late fifties, stood the moment she swept into the door. His face lit with a smile as he waved her over to his table.

"Hi," she said, holding out her hand. "I hope you haven't been waiting long."

"Just a few minutes." His green-eyed gaze swept over her in appreciation. "You look lovely this morning."

Zya certainly hadn't gone out of her way to dress up for the date she'd never asked for. She was wearing her usual uniform of a long, flowing dress with lace-up boots, and she had her dark hair tied back into a long ponytail. "Um, thanks. You look nice, too."

Her statement wasn't a lie. Objectively, Charles was a handsome man. He had curious green eyes, a strong jaw, and wavy silver hair that was lush and stylish. His fitted jeans and long-sleeved thermal shirt made it obvious the man took care of himself. She imagined there were a lot of ladies in Keating Hollow who would consider him a catch. And while he was a good bit older than her, that wasn't the problem. Her problem was that she saw herself with someone else. Someone who looked a lot like her best friend, Brody Saxon.

"Thank you." He waved for her to take a seat at his table. "Can I get you a coffee or something to eat before we go?"

Zya glanced over at the counter and smiled at Hanna, the owner. Hanna raised her eyebrows in question as she glanced at Charles and then back at Zya. Zya gave her a small shake of her head and turned her attention back to Charles. "Sure. I'd love a Chai latte and a piece of lemon pound cake." She reached into her bag, pulling out her wallet.

"I've got it," Charles said quickly and hurried over to the counter to place the order.

The bell on the front door chimed, playing an instrumental version of what sounded a lot like "Love Shack" by the B-52s. Zya chuckled to herself. The choice was left over from Valentine's Day. Apparently the café was going to celebrate all month long.

"I thought you said you were headed out with friends today?" Brody said, suddenly standing next to her table, his eyes full of suspicion as he stared down at her.

She glanced up at him, frowning. "What?" She shook her head. "Why are you checking up on me?"

"I'm not. I stopped in for coffee before heading into work and spotted you with that guy." He jerked a thumb at Charles. "It looks an awful lot like you're on a date."

Zya felt her cheeks flush with heat. She didn't know why she hadn't just told Brody her aunts interfered to set her up on a date with Charles. It wasn't like this was going to turn into anything. She'd just felt uncomfortable about the entire thing, and when he'd asked where she was headed this morning, she'd said the first thing that came to mind. "Well, it's a date with a new friend, I guess. My aunts set it up. Sort of."

He raised both his eyebrows "Your aunts? Again?"

She threw up her hands. "Yes. Again. They are relentless. Regardless, why are you so irritated? Is it because you have to work on a Sunday?" The winery held an event once a month to help encourage sales during the off season. It meant all hands on deck. It also meant that Winnie was spending the day with Wanda's sister again. Apparently the two had hit it off, and Blake had offered to watch the little girl when her schedule permitted.

"No. That's not it at all." He shook his head. "You know I don't really care what days I work. It's—" He glanced over at Charles and narrowed his eyes. "I just don't see you with someone like him. He's too—"

"Old?" Zya asked with a small smile on her lips as she held in a laugh.

"Yes. No. He's just not your type." Brody crossed his arms over his chest and pressed his lips together, looking petulant.

"What's my type?" Zya asked, curious to hear what he'd say.

"I don't know. Someone who can keep up with you when you head out on your long walks in the woods. Who can go toe-to-toe with you when you binge a pizza. Who will be at

57

your side when you're old and gray and who will rub your hands when you complain about your arthritis."

Amused, Zya grinned at him. "You know who that sounds like, right?"

"Someone who isn't pushing sixty?" he asked, not bothering to hide his irritation.

She snickered and then sobered when Charles appeared at the table with their drinks.

"Hello," he said to Brody. "Are you a friend of Zya's?"

Brody gave the man a sharp nod, but didn't say anything.

"Charles, this is my best friend Brody. Brody, this is Charles. My date."

Charles put the drinks down and held his hand out to Brody. "It's really nice to meet you. Are you joining us?"

"No," Zya said quickly. "Brody's on his way to work. Right, Brody?"

Brody tore his gaze from Charles and focused on Zya, who just grinned at him. "Yes, but I have a few minutes." He grabbed a nearby chair and sat right next to Zya so that he could stare down her date. "So, Charles, tell me about yourself."

Charles blinked a few times, seeming a little bit startled that Brody had just crashed their date, despite the fact that he'd invited Brody only a moment ago. "Um, well, I own a lumber yard just outside of town, but I'm semi-retired—"

"Retired?" Brody interrupted. "That's interesting. What do you spend your days doing now? Pickleball?"

Zya snorted her laughter and then covered with a cough, hoping Charles didn't think she was laughing at him. He seemed like a nice enough man. It wasn't his fault she wasn't even remotely interested in him.

"Actually, yes. They have courts down at the Keating

Hollow fitness center. It turns out pickleball is a fun sport," Charles said. "Do you play?"

"No," Brody said, giving Zya a look that said, *see, I told you he was too old for you.*

Charles took a sip of his coffee and then leaned forward. "Zip, my hockey buddy, turned me onto it last year when he was visiting from Vancouver. By the second game, I was hooked."

"Zip McLaughlin? The star forward for the Vancouver Spellcasters? That hockey friend?" Brody asked.

Charles chuckled. "Yeah, that's Zip. He comes to Keating Hollow to visit family a couple times a year."

"Hmm," Zya said, tapping her chin. "I guess if Zip is a fan, then pickleball might be cooler than you think it is, Brody." She grinned at him, enjoying that Charles had just put him in his place. It was Brody's fault for acting like an agist fool.

"I never said pickleball wasn't cool," Brody mumbled. When no one answered him, he straightened his shoulders and pierced Charles with his penetrating gaze. "Listen. I'll just get straight to the point and say that Zya is my best friend, a respected business woman, and basically the coolest person I know. She's not someone to be used while some older man is going through his midlife crisis. So if that's what this is, then I suggest you get up and leave now. Because she deserves more than some guy who just wants to relive his glory days."

"Brody!" Zya jumped to her feet and grabbed him by the ear, yanking him from his chair.

"Ouch! Son of a… Dammit, Zya let go." He was bent over sideways, shuffling behind her as she tugged him toward the front door.

"Not until we're outside where I can give you a piece of my mind," she said through clenched teeth.

He let out a groan, but didn't struggle.

Once they were on the cobblestone sidewalk, she released him and stood with her hands on her hips, glaring up at him. "Just what in the fresh hell was that, Brody Saxon? I can't believe how incredibly rude you were back there. You basically admonished a man you don't even know for taking me out on a date. Not to mention you accused him of trying to use me for sex. Not cool, Brody. Not cool. At. All."

Brody's Adam's apple bobbed as he swallowed. A muscle in his jaw ticked with tension.

She pointed a finger at him and poked him in the chest. "I don't know what's gotten into you, but I'm a grown-ass woman who doesn't need you to act like an overprotective, overbearing father figure. Explain yourself."

"I…" He ran a hand through his hair, looking frustrated. "I can't. I don't know what came over me."

She raised an accusatory eyebrow. "You don't know? There's obviously some reason why you went full-on jackass back there."

He blew out a long breath. "I guess I just don't want to see you get hurt again. After Carter—"

She held up a hand, stopping him. "My date today has nothing to do with Carter."

"Are you sure?" he asked softly.

"Stop, Brody," she said, all the heat gone from her tone. "I don't need you acting like I'm so broken by what Carter did that I've started making questionable choices. It's just one date. I'm not shacking up with the man or marrying him. For goddess's sake, I don't even know if I like him. And what you did in there was just plain rude. I'm a grown woman. I make the decisions about what's best for me. Got it?"

"Got it." He held his hands up and took a step back. When

he dropped them, he rubbed the back of his neck and said, "I'm sorry. I know that was uncalled for. It's just that I'm protective."

"There's a huge difference between being protective and just being a jackass," she said, more irritated than ever by his actions. She didn't want him to act like her big brother. Like he was going to beat down any suitor who would take advantage of her. Besides, he had no room to cast stones. The man standing in front of her had knocked someone up on a one-night stand and then moved on, causing him to miss years of his daughter's life. Had she mentioned any of that? Had she berated him for his reckless choices? No. They'd been his mistakes to make and his to rectify. "You aren't exactly a saint when it comes to how you run your love life, Brody Saxon. Remember that the next time you dress down someone else for their choices."

"Zya—"

"No," she said quietly. "We're done here. I'm going back to my date. Go to work. I'll see you tonight." She turned, ready to head back into the café.

"I'm sorry, Zy."

Without turning around, she nodded and then strode back inside.

CHAPTER 8

"Your friend seems a little protective," Charles said when Zya took her seat across from him.

She let out a humorless laugh. "You can say that again."

"Is there something going on there that I should know about?" he asked, glancing over his shoulder toward the front door.

"No." She shook her head. "We've never been anything more than friends. I'm really sorry about that. He was way out of line."

Charles gave her a slow nod as he said, "He was, but I guess if I were in his shoes, I might be a little jealous, too."

"He's not jealous," she said adamantly. "It's really not like that."

"Maybe not for you, but it is for him." Charles pushed a small plate that had a slice of lemon pound cake toward her. "Can't say I blame him. He's right. You do seem like just about the coolest person around."

She sighed, deciding to ignore his latest remark about Brody. It wasn't worth arguing about.

"Listen, Zya," Charles said, clasping his hands together. "I know you didn't really want to go on this date. Your aunt seemed really sincere when she said she just really wanted you to get out of the house. She said you hadn't made that many friends since moving here, but I can see that's not really true, is it?"

"No, it's not," Zya agreed. "Besides Brody, I've made friends with some of the women here in town."

He nodded. "I caught that when Hanna asked about you when I was up at the counter ordering. We don't have to finish the date if you don't want to. It wasn't really fair of me or your aunt to push you into this."

Zya sat back in her chair, feeling a little stunned. He was right. She hadn't wanted to go on this date, but she'd gone through with it because of some sort of ingrained politeness. But still, she felt rejected. It wasn't that she was particularly interested in dating Charles, but she didn't want to feel like she was so uninteresting that she was being given the brushoff before she even finished her coffee. "Was it something I said?" she asked with a chuckle. "I mean, I was sort of looking forward to the car show." That was the truth. Zya liked vintage sports cars.

Charles beamed at her. "If you're up for it, so am I." He stood and held out his hand to her. "Ready?"

Zya let him help her up and then chuckled when he draped her coat over her shoulders. "It's been a while since I've been out with a gentleman."

"Stick with me, Zya. I'll show you what it means to be treated right." He winked and led her out of the café.

"I'M gonna need to get me a vintage 1958 Corvette," Zya said as she climbed out of Charles's 1969 Charger. "That is quite possibly the sexiest car ever made."

Charles grinned at her. "I can't think of another car more appropriate for you."

She laughed. They'd had a great time at the car show. Charles's Charger had even won an award. He'd been charming and attentive and had included her in every conversation, never once assuming that she didn't know anything about cars. It had been refreshing. When was the last time she'd been on a date when the guy had treated her as an equal? Not like Carter, who'd somehow always assumed he knew more than her about every subject and tried to mansplain everything until Zya shut him down.

She sighed to herself. What exactly had she seen in Carter? The further she got away from that relationship, the more she wondered what the hell she'd been thinking.

"Is everything okay?" Charles asked her.

"Huh?" She glanced over at him and then gave him a sheepish smile. "Yeah. It's all good. I was just thinking about... never mind. It doesn't matter. Not when we have wine to taste." She started to walk toward the barn, where the Pelshes had set up their tasting room.

"Oh, we're not here to taste wines. Or at least not yet," he said, grinning. "There's a dance contest."

Zya stopped in her tracks. "A dance contest?"

"Yep. It's a fundraiser for Creative Kids, the new art and music program that Austin Steele and Gideon Alexander opened this year. It's been so successful that there's interest in opening another one up in Bafana Bay."

"Befana Bay?" Zya asked. "Where's that?"

"Up north in Washington. Turns out Silas Ansell is filming there right now. Gideon and Miranda were up there for book signing a few months ago, and one thing led to another. Now they're trying to raise money to open another location. Kinda cool, I think. There's nothing better than encouraging kids to be creative."

"Ah, yes. I agree." Zya had heard of Silas Ansell of course. His sister, Shannon Knox, who also happened to be his agent, lived in town. But so far, she hadn't met the young star. She had been present during the Academy Awards party last year when he'd won his best actor award, and it had been quite the celebration. It turned out that Silas and his budding-rock star boyfriend, Levi Kelley, were deeply loved in the town of Keating Hollow.

"So you'll do it with me, then? I have sponsors who've already pledged."

Zya stared into his bright eyes and didn't know how she could possibly refuse. A dance contest was just about the last thing she wanted to do, but it was for charity, right? "I'll do it, but I think I'm gonna need a glass of wine or two to get me started."

He laughed, took her by the hand, and started to guide her toward a large event tent that was set up where they usually held the outdoor weddings. "Pretty sure that's not going to be an issue."

"Charles!" An older woman with white hair grabbed him by the arm the moment he and Zya slipped into the tent. "You made it. I was wondering if we'd see you."

"Ms. Betty. Hello," he said kindly. "Not only am I here, but I managed to get some sponsors for the event."

"Well, that's lovely," she said, eyeing him up and down. "You wouldn't happen to need a dance partner, would you?"

He chuckled. "No. Zya here has already agreed."

"That's a real shame," she said, looking disappointed as she turned her attention to Zya, frowning. But then she quickly smiled and winked at Zya. "Looks like you've managed to snag Keating Hollow's most eligible bachelor. Lucky you."

Zya let out a cough, covering a chuckle of her own. "Charles and I are just friends."

"Isn't that what they all say, dear?" Ms. Betty pumped her eyebrows suggestively.

"How about I save a dance for you Saturday night at the brewery," Charles asked Betty. "We can show the young ones how it's done."

"I'm going to hold you to that," she said, patting his chest.

"Oh, I know you will," Charles said.

Zya watched the sassy older woman sashay away, swinging her hips wildly. "She's going to throw her back out if she keeps that up."

Charles snickered. "I wouldn't put any money on that. Ms. Betty is a tough old bird."

"She's fabulous," Zya said with obvious admiration. "That's who I want to be at that age."

After grabbing a couple of glasses of wine, they didn't have to wait long until Ms. Betty stood up at the podium and ordered everyone to line up on the dance floor. The music started and the next thing Zya knew, she was being twirled around in a frenzy, barely managing to keep up with her much more experienced dance partner.

They danced three rounds before Zya stopped and doubled over as she clutched the cramp in her side. "I need a break," she huffed.

"I'll fill in." An auburn-haired woman who looked to be in her late fifties had appeared out of nowhere.

Charles's eyes lit with obvious interest. "Celeste. I didn't know you were back in town."

She smiled brightly. "I just got in last night. Ms. Betty told me about the dance contest, but I didn't have any time to find a partner." The woman turned to Zya. "You don't mind, do you?"

"Not at all," Zya said, waving a hand toward Charles. "Please, take my place. I need water or maybe a stretcher," she joked. "He's far too advanced for this novice."

Celeste patted her arm kindly and then took her place in Charles's arms.

Zya hobbled over to the refreshment table, grabbed a bottle of water, and then took a seat at one of the tables set up off to the side of the dance floor. The music started up again, and she watched as Charles and Celeste moved across the dance floor as if they were Fred and Ginger.

"They're pretty impressive, aren't they?" Brody said, sitting in a seat beside her.

She glanced over at her friend. "How long have you been here?"

"Long enough to see that you still have two left feet," he teased.

Zya laughed. "I wasn't that bad."

He shrugged. "Maybe not. But you're no match for *Charrrles.*" He dragged out her date's name and then smirked like a twelve-year-old.

"Jealousy really isn't a good look on you," she said mildly, suddenly thinking that maybe Charles had been right in his assessment. Brody was acting like he was jealous. What else would explain his obnoxious behavior?

That sobered him quickly. "You think I'm jealous?"

She shrugged one shoulder. "What would you call it? You were pretty brutal this morning at the café."

"I'm not jealous. I just want the best for you," he insisted as he stood and held his hand out to her. "Come on. Let me take you for a spin around the dance floor."

"Are you serious?" she asked.

"Of course I am." He wrapped his hand around hers and tugged.

Zya let him lead her to the dance floor. After he slipped his arms around her waist, she stared up at him, her eyes narrowed. "If you weren't jealous, then why were you acting like an overbearing jackass this morning?"

"It's just obvious that he isn't the right guy for you."

Zya pulled back slightly to get a better look at him. "Who is the right guy for me, Brody?"

He stared down at her as he started to move back and forth, so that they swayed to the music. "You need someone who understands you, Zya. Someone who celebrates your independence, your fierceness, and your passion for life. Not someone who is interested in making you conform to what they want."

"You think Charles wanted me to be something I'm not? You barely even met the guy. I'll have you know that today was probably the best date I've had in… well, maybe ever. You have no idea what you're talking about," she said, offended. Who was Brody to decide who she should date?

"The best date ever?" he asked, looking shocked. "Are you saying this is a real thing? That you're into him?" His eyes were wide and full of shock, as if that wasn't something he'd really considered. But then something that looked a lot like sadness flashed in his brilliant blue eyes before it quickly vanished and turned to concern.

"No. I'm not. I just met him," she said carefully, not sure what else to say. She hated his snap judgment of Charles. It just wasn't like her friend to act so hostile. "What is it about Charles that you don't like? Is it just his age or…"

"I don't know. Maybe. Usually older guys like that date younger women to make themselves look better. I don't want anyone to ever treat you like that."

"That's awfully judgmental, considering you don't even know him. And ageist," she said quietly. "I get why you'd think that, but I don't think it's true for Charles. He truly was interested in what I had to say and has been a complete gentleman."

"If you say so, Zy. I just want you to be happy. If it's this guy, then I'll pack away my garbage and be supportive."

She reached up and cupped his cheek. "Thank you for saying that, but Charles and I aren't a match. He's a nice guy, but there's zero spark there."

He looked visibly relieved as he took in her words. Pulling her in closer, he whispered, "I just want better for you. After Carter, you deserve someone special. Someone who will treat you like the goddess you are."

"You're biased," she said, feeling a little raw. Why couldn't her perfect match just be Brody? He understood her. Always had.

"Definitely," he said, pulling back again and giving her a soft smile. "But that doesn't change the fact that you deserve so much better than Carter. He never appreciated your uniqueness. He only saw you as an extension of him. Your accomplishments made him look good, and he liked that. Instead of being proud to be by your side, he made everything about him. As if your success as a talented witch who turned your family's herb shop into an international phenomenon somehow was because of him. As if he'd had anything to do with that. But he'd tell anyone who listened that your ideas were his."

"He did?" she asked, knowing she shouldn't be shocked by that revelation. At this point, she wouldn't put anything past her ex. He'd turned out to be a manipulative SOB who hid behind his natural charm. It had taken her far too long to see past his façade. Prior to moving to Keating Hollow, Zya had managed her family's herbal business in Salem. She'd taken it from a small operation that was mostly visited by tourists to one that supplied stock to stores around the world. When she decided she had to leave town after her breakup with Carter, she'd left a thriving business in her cousins' capable hands.

"Yes. When you two were in Paris a few years ago, he tried to rope Miss Francine into investing in his startup. He claimed he coached you on how to turn around your family business. When she came to me to ask what I thought, I laid it out for her, and told her in no uncertain terms that Carter couldn't find his ass even if he had a herd of donkeys and to skip it."

Zya snorted. "If he had a herd of donkeys? Nice one, Brody."

He pulled her in close, hugging her, and Zya couldn't help melting into him.

She still couldn't believe that she'd agreed to marry Carter. He'd done a thorough job of conning her and everyone else she knew. Though deep down, she knew he wasn't right for her. She supposed she'd been trying to love someone other than her best friend. That had been an epic fail. "I'm glad you're here, Brody."

"I'm glad I'm here too, Zya. I've missed you."

She hugged him tighter, holding onto those words with everything she had.

When the song ended, they moved off the dance floor. While Brody went to get them a bottle of water, she watched Charles and Celeste dance circles around everyone else. There was no doubt that if they stayed partnered, they'd win without any trouble.

Charles spotted her, said something to Celeste, and hurried over to her. "I'm sorry. I didn't mean to leave you by yourself."

"I'm not by myself," she said, waving at Brody, who was already walking toward them. "Besides, I think it's obvious you and Celeste need to finish out this contest together. You two are something else on the dance floor."

His lips curved into a smile as he glanced over at the other woman. She was getting her own bottle of water and eyeing him like a hawk. No way was Celeste letting him out of her sight. "I'm here with you," he said without looking at Zya.

She laughed and placed a hand on his forearm. "I think it's obvious to the entire town that you want to be here with her. Go on. I'll get Brody to give me a ride."

Charles finally cut his gaze to her. "Are you sure?"

"I'm positive. Now go on before someone else snatches her up. I think we both know she's who you really want to be with."

He gave her a grateful smile. "You're a really good date. You know that, Zya?"

Grinning, she shook her head. "Nah. Just a friend who can see when she's in the way." She gave him a gentle nudge. A moment later Celeste nodded a thanks in Zya's direction.

"That was a nice thing you did," Brody said, handing her a fresh bottle of water.

"As fun as a dance contest is," she said, not bothering to hide her sarcasm, "I think I'm ready to call it a day. You're not headed home any time soon, are you?"

"As a matter of fact, I clocked out about ten minutes before I started twirling you around this tent." He held his hand out to her. "I'm ready to go if you are."

Zya slipped her hand into his and then hugged his arm as they made their way out of the tent. "Do me a favor, will you?"

"What's that, Zy?"

"Never let me forget to put my guards up so that my aunts can't ambush me again. Charles was a nice man, but I'm not interested in being set up on any more blind dates. In fact, I think I'm going to get a couple more cats and become a spinster."

He paused and gazed down at her, his eyes sweeping over her. "I'll remind you about your aunts, but spinster? No way. You've got far too much passion hiding under that mysterious witchy persona of yours. One day, Zy, you're gonna find your match. And when you do, it's going to be explosive."

"I wish I had your optimism. So far the only dates I've been on were with a rocker who was in town for less than a week and a man older than my father. I'd say I'm striking out in the dating department."

Brody paused just before he got to his truck. "You forgot date number three."

She raised both eyebrows. "Do you know something I don't?"

He winked at her. "Tonight, you've got a date with your best friend and your goddaughter. I'd say things are looking up."

Warmth spread through Zya's chest as she smiled up at him. "I can't wait."

CHAPTER 9

*B*rody glanced over at Zya, taking in her delicate features as she sat in the passenger seat, staring out the window. The sun was starting to set, causing her face to glow in the evening light. He couldn't remember ever seeing her look so beautiful before.

"Stop staring at me and go," she said without looking at him. "The light is green."

"I'm not staring," he muttered as he focused on the road again. Dammit. Why couldn't he stop staring at Zya? Ever since he'd seen her with that Charles dude, he'd been irritated. And yes, if he was honest with himself, he was jealous. He'd acted like an idiot. Brody had no business telling her who she shouldn't be dating. It was just that watching her date people he knew weren't right for her made his gut ache.

He pulled into the long driveway that led to Wanda and Cameron's home. They'd built a lovely place just outside of town a few years ago that they called Copeland Farm. Blake, Wanda's half sister, lived in an apartment attached to the garage. As soon as Brody put the truck into park, the door to the apartment popped open and Winnie ran out, her arms held high as she made a beeline for the vehicle.

Brody jumped out of the truck and quickly scooped her up, swinging her around while she let out a whoop of delight.

Blake followed behind her and stood with her hands in her jean pockets as she watched them.

"Did you have a good time?" Brody asked his daughter as he set her on her feet.

She nodded vigorously. "We made cookies!"

No wonder she had so much energy. He glanced over at Blake. "How many did she have?"

"Just a couple," Blake said, looking sheepish. "I did feed her dinner first though."

Zya stepped up beside him and was nearly knocked over when Winnie slammed into her legs, hugging them for all she was worth. "Whoa, little princess. What's going on?"

Winnie just grinned up at Zya, her wide eyes sparkling with joy.

"Clearly she had a good time," Brody said, pulling out his wallet so that he could pay Blake.

"I think she might have snuck a cookie or two more than I allotted," Blake confessed. "I swear, you can't even blink around her sometimes. Girl is quite the cookie snatcher."

"She is," Brody agreed. "Don't worry about it. She's happy, so I'm happy." He handed Blake the cash and then patted her shoulder before he turned to scoop up his daughter, but as soon as he reached for her, she ran off back toward the garage.

"Winnie!" Zya raced after her.

Brody watched them both, completely amused. He waved at Blake as she made her way back into her apartment and then followed Zya and Winnie. His heart completely melted when he rounded the building and found them both sitting in a purple golf cart, Zya at the wheel with Winnie in her lap. His daughter was gripping the steering wheel and moving her hands back and forth as if she were weaving in and out of traffic.

"Uh-oh, Dad," Wanda said conspiratorially as she approached them. "I think Winnie has caught the golf cart racing bug."

"Golf cart!" Winnie called out, beaming at him.

All he could do was laugh. "I'm pretty sure it's going to be a while before it's legal for my little one to start racing golf carts."

"You'd be surprised." Wanda gave him an exaggerated wink. She turned her attention to Zya. "We missed you at the last race. Are you interested in joining us Thursday for girls' night?"

Zya glanced at Brody and then down at Winnie before she started to shake her head.

"She'll be there," Brody answered for her, knowing she was declining because of them. "Where and when?"

"Brody! I can answer for myself," Zya insisted.

"No, you can't, because it appears you were going to decline just to sit at home with me and eat spaghetti. I won't have it. You go spend time with your friends and bring back a blue ribbon."

"Blue ribbon?" Wanda and Zya asked at the same time. They eyed each other and then started laughing. "From where?" Wanda gasped out between chuckles. "How is Zya going to secure a blue ribbon?"

"Winning the golf cart race?" he asked.

They both started sputtering with laughter.

"There's no blue ribbon, Brody," Wanda said, wiping her eyes. "We race for real stakes. You know, things like paying for spa days, or having to detail someone else's golf cart. Or my personal favorite, the loser has to drive down Main Street blasting "Loser" by Beck."

"Really? This is what you're exposing my innocent daughter to?" he asked, even more amused than ever. He really liked Wanda. She was both fun and joyful while being really good at her job. She'd managed to negotiate the deal for the property he wanted without a huge back and forth. Both parties seemed to be happy and closing was on schedule to be finalized within thirty days. He couldn't have asked for a better Realtor.

"It's best to train them young, Brody." Wanda turned to Zya. "Don't you agree?"

"Absolutely," Zya said. "She's gonna be the baddest toddler Keating Hollow's preschool has ever seen."

Brody turned his gaze skyward. "I'm going to be in some serious trouble, aren't I?"

Wanda and Zya cackled, and then Zya called, "Come on, Dad. Get in. We'll take you for a spin around the property."

"We should probably get going—"

"Stop being a party pooper," Wanda insisted as she climbed in the back. "Get in so I can show you something."

Curious, Brody did as he was told and watched as Zya strapped her and Winnie in with the same seatbelt.

"Let's go, cutie," she whispered to Winnie as she gently pressed on the pedal, making the cart inch forward. "Keep a tight grip on the wheel and do as I say, okay?"

Winnie stared up at Zya with wide eyes and nodded, fully entranced by the gorgeous woman.

So was Brody. Zya was being so careful and kind with his daughter. Yeah, she probably shouldn't be riding on Zya's lap as she drove, but they weren't going more than a few miles an hour, and it wasn't like they were on city streets. They were just rolling down the dirt path on Wanda's property.

"We're going to turn that way now," Zya said, pointing to the path that veered toward the left. "Turn the steering wheel like this." Zya showed her how to move the wheel to make the cart go in the direction they desired.

Winnie did exactly as Zya did, and when the cart moved down the path, Winnie let go and clapped, clearly delighted.

Zya chuckled. "Don't let go, sweetie pie. You don't want the cart to head off into the ditch, do you?"

Winnie grabbed the wheel again, but at no point had they been in danger of going into any ditch or anywhere else that would be problematic. Zya had a firm grip on the wheel and had been in charge the entire time, just making Winnie think she was driving.

Brody watched the pair with his heart in his throat. No one else in his life had made an effort to connect with his daughter the way Zya had. Since the day she'd come to live with him, he'd felt like it was him and Winnie against the world. His parents, while they talked a good game about wanting her in their lives, had barely spent more than ten minutes with her when they'd been in Salem. His old friends hadn't come around. They'd acted horrified by his new circumstances.

He'd thought once he moved back to Salem that he'd have some sort of support. That had proven to be a foolish thought almost immediately. Brody should have known that his parents' solution to everything was to hire multiple nannies while expecting him to live with them and follow their rules, which included working for his father. It didn't matter that Brody was an accomplished vintner or that he was in high demand for his skills. They'd just wanted what they wanted, regardless of what Brody wanted for his life.

It was why he'd taken the Keating Hollow job without even really looking anywhere else. He'd known deep in his soul that Zya would be there for him and Winnie. He hadn't expected to move in with her, even temporarily, but he had known that she'd be the emotional support that he needed. She'd always been that person for him. And now, the way she was with Winnie just made him love her more.

"Step on it, Zya!" Wanda called from the back seat.

Zya let out a whoop and sped up a smidge, pretending they were flying along the trail.

Winnie mimicked her, and the two of them were alight with joy.

Brody clutched his heart, knowing that this moment was one he'd never forget.

At some point, Wanda reached across from the back seat and flipped a switch. Purple and white lights lit up the cart and music started blaring from the speakers. Both Wanda and Zya started singing along to "Party in the USA" while Winnie wiggled in Zya's lap, dancing along with them.

"Come on, Brody," Zya called to him. "Get in on this party. Either sing or dance, or both."

Winnie turned to him. "Dance, Daddy!"

He chuckled and lifted his hands like he was raising the roof and then mimicked his daughter's wiggling as they danced in unison.

Zya glanced over at him, her eyes sparkling as she let out a loud laugh before turning her attention back to the path.

"Right there!" Wanda pointed to an area to the right. "By the tree."

Zya steered the cart over to the tree and once the vehicle was parked, they all jumped out.

"Look over there," Wanda said, pointing down the hill. "See that house over there past the river?"

Brody took a few steps and shielded his eyes against the fading sunset. He scanned the area and then locked his gaze on his new home. He turned to Wanda. "You didn't tell me we were going to be neighbors."

She smirked. "Well, not exactly neighbors. There's public land between us, but close enough I guess."

"There's a bridge about a half mile that way," Zya said, pointing to the east as she spoke to Wanda. "A foot bridge, so you won't even have to drive when Brody invites you over for his first winetasting."

"Yes!" Wanda pumped her fist in the air. "Score!"

The adults all chuckled while Winnie ran back to the golf cart and jumped into the driver's seat. Brody said a silent prayer of thanks that her feet couldn't reach the pedals. He could just see her taking off and leaving them all behind.

"We'd better go," Wanda said, slipping her arm through Brody's. "It's going to get dark soon, and I'm sure you want to get the little one home."

"Yeah. Seven is going to come awfully early tomorrow," he said, already dreading taking her to preschool. He hated the idea of leaving her for the first time at a new school where she knew no one.

"It's gonna be okay, Dad," Wanda said softly. "The preschool here in Keating Hollow is really good. You're going to love it. I promise."

He'd gotten the school recommendation from Wanda, who seemed to know everyone and everything that had to do with Keating Hollow. She'd been a godsend to be honest. "It's just hard."

"Understandable." Wanda led him to the golf cart and

stopped beside Winnie. "Scoot over, cutie pie. It's my turn to drive. Want to sit next to me and play DJ?"

Winnie looked up at her in confusion but didn't complain when Brody reached for her and pulled her out of the driver's seat. "How about we sit in the back and play thumb wars?"

"Okay," she said simply. And the moment they were settled, she held her fist out with her thumb up, waiting to start the game.

Brody grinned at his little girl, held his fist out to her, and immediately let her trap his thumb beneath hers. He'd learned pretty quickly that if he played with her and let her win, he could occupy her for hours. He'd gladly throw every game they ever played as long as she was having a good time.

"Goodness. He's a natural," Wanda said to Zya.

Zya eyed them and nodded. "Yes, he is."

Pride swelled in Brody's chest. He'd come a long way in the past couple of months. He'd gone from carefree bachelor to doting dad on the turn of a dime, and he was damned proud of himself. While he knew his daughter would need help navigating the loss of her mother, she was adjusting as well as anyone could hope, nonetheless.

He knew without a doubt that coming to Keating Hollow had been the best choice he'd ever made.

When Wanda stepped on the accelerator, it was suddenly clear why she insisted on driving. There was no more five miles an hour. They were flying down the trail, the wind in their hair as they chased the daylight. Thumb wars were off the table due to the bumpy ride, so Brody wrapped his arm around his daughter and held her close all the way back to the house.

By the time Wanda parked the golf cart in front of the garage, Winnie's eyes were drooping, and he knew as soon as he got her into her car seat she'd be out like a light. Sure enough, ten minutes later when they were on their way to get Zya's car, he glanced in the rearview mirror and spotted his daughter's head lolling to the side. He let out a soft chuckle.

"What is it?" Zya asked softly.

"My kid slays me. One minute she's in hyperdrive and the next she's out like a light."

Zya glanced back at Winnie. "I wish I slept that well."

"You and me both. I'm only out like that after—" Brody quickly clamped his mouth shut and shook his head. "Never mind."

Zya let out a laugh, clearly having guessed what he'd been about to say. "I'd imagine there hasn't been much female company since Short-stuff showed up."

"None. Zero. Zip," he confirmed. "But honestly, Zy, I don't mind. She's far more important than a meaningless hookup."

"You're right. She is," Zya confirmed. She turned serious eyes on him, and when she opened her mouth, he was certain she was going to give him some sort of lecture about his love life. But instead, she said, "I always knew you'd be a great dad. And look at you. You're killing it, Brode."

Her praise hit him hard in the gut, and he felt his eyes get hot with unshed tears. What the hell was that? He had to get it together before he had to pull over and sob into her neck. Brody blinked back the tears and in a gruff voice, he forced out, "Thanks, Zy."

She reached over and squeezed his leg, and when she removed her hand, his leg tingled from her touch.

He nearly groaned, desperately wishing that she'd touch him again. Everywhere.

"It's right there," Zya said, pointing to her Jeep that was parked a few doors down from Incantation Café.

He quickly pulled in beside her Jeep, and as she climbed out, he said, "I'll see you back at home."

"Home. Right," she said with a nod, and her lips curved into a pleased smile.

He knew she loved having them at her place. It was obvious every time he called her house home. He just hoped they didn't overstay their welcome. Having a three-year-old around was a lot more than she'd bargained for.

After waiting for her to get into her Jeep and back out of her spot, he followed her back to her house. The moment they pulled into her drive, he frowned when he spotted the black SUV that was parked on the street out front. It hadn't been there when he left that morning. And none of the houses were that close that someone would park right there for no reason.

His body was practically vibrating with tension when he slammed his truck into park and jumped out. He scanned the area, certain that someone was there.

"Brody? What's wrong?" Zya said, hurrying to his side.

"I don't know. Can you get Winnie, please?"

"Of course." She quickly opened the back door of the crew cab and went to work on releasing the child restraints.

Footsteps sounded from the porch as boots clambered across the wood. A moment later, a tall man wearing a dark police uniform appeared from the shadows.

"Drew?" Zya called from behind Brody. "What's going on?"

The deputy sheriff tipped his hat toward her. "Sorry to bother you, Zya. I have something for Mr. Saxon."

"Me?" Brody stared at the law enforcement officer with confusion, having no idea what business he had with him.

"Brody Saxon?" Drew asked him as he walked off the porch toward them.

"The one and only," Brody said. "What can I help you with, Officer?"

"I'm sorry to be meeting for the first time under these circumstances, Mr. Saxon. I'm Deputy Drew Baker and unfortunately, you've been served." Drew held out a large manilla envelope.

Brody reflexively took the envelope but wasn't sure he'd heard the man correctly. "Served? As in I'm being sued?"

Drew gave him a curt nod. "It appears so. Again, I am sorry. I hope we meet under better conditions soon."

As Drew walked down the drive to his SUV, Brody stared at the envelope in his hand, wondering who the hell would be suing him. And for what, exactly?

"Come on," Zya said, leading the way up the porch with Winnie in her arms. His daughter had her arms and legs wrapped around Zya, her head resting on Zya's shoulder.

If Brody hadn't just been served, he'd probably have melted at the sight. Instead, he was vibrating with anxiety. How had anyone even found him at Zya's house? As soon as he stepped into the house, he tossed the envelope onto her entry table, held his hands out for Winnie, and once Zya handed her over, he took her to her room to get her ready for bed.

His girl was a limp noodle when he finally poured her into her bed. After tucking PJ into her arms and kissing her on the cheek, he retreated back to the living room where he found Zya sitting on the couch with two open beers.

She held one out to him. "I thought you might need this."

Brody eyed it. "Whiskey would probably be the better choice."

"I thought so, too. But this is all I have." She grimaced. "Sorry."

He closed his eyes as he shook his head. Then he took a

long pull, draining nearly half the bottle before setting it down and tearing into the envelope.

Brody stared at the papers in his hand and then slowly sank into a chair across from his friend. His brain was having trouble processing the words.

Without saying a word, Zya got up and walked over to him. She carefully took the papers from him and scanned them, and then Brody could have sworn he saw steam coming out of her ears. "They can't do this!" she roared. "They have no right!"

It was her pure rage that somehow seemed to calm him. He gently took the papers from her and stared down at the words he hadn't been able to comprehend before.

But there it was in black and white.

His parents were suing for custody of his daughter.

CHAPTER 10

*Z*ya sat in the lawyer's office, holding Brody's hand. It had been two days since they'd come home to find Drew on her porch, waiting to serve Brody those damned papers. She'd known Brody's parents for most of her life, and while she'd been aware that they were selfish A-holes, she'd never imagined that they'd do something so horrible.

For the life of her, she just couldn't imagine why they'd sue for custody. Brody was an excellent father. One only had to watch him for five minutes with Winnie to come to that conclusion. But she imagined that they hadn't spent any time observing him with his daughter. They likely just told him what they wanted him to do and then ignored him and Winnie completely until they up and left.

"Give it to me straight, Lorna" Brody said to the no-nonsense lawyer sitting behind her desk. Her silver hair was twisted into a severe bun and her wire-rimmed glasses were positioned at the end of her nose as she eyed the file. "Do they have a case?"

The lawyer pulled her glasses off and laid them on her desk.

Leaning forward, she clasped her hands together. "Normally, I'd say absolutely not. But this case is a bit unusual for a couple of reasons."

"What reasons are those?" Zya couldn't stop herself from asking. "Brody is Winnie's father, and he's done nothing to demonstrate that he's not able to take care of her. This is complete BS."

"Personally, Ms. Rossi, I completely agree with you," the lawyer said, her expression stony. "Unfortunately, there is reason to worry about which way the judge will rule on this case. The fact that the child's mother has died and Mr. Saxon did not have a relationship with Winnie up until about two months ago could sway the outcome."

"That's wasn't my choice," Brody said, his tone even, almost void of emotion.

Zya wondered how he was keeping it together. If she were in his shoes, she'd have been on the phone to her parents giving them a tongue lashing they wouldn't soon forget. Instead, Brody had gone no contact with his parents, even going so far as to refuse to answer their persistent calls over the past two days.

"I understand that," Lorna said, her expression softening as she spoke to Brody. "Hopefully the judge will take that into consideration, but if we get one who is big on traditional family values, they could rule that it's better for Winnie to have both a mother and a father."

"That's complete—" Zya started.

The lawyer held up her hand, cutting Zya off. "However, since the two of you are together and sharing a house, if you can satisfy the judge that you're in a committed relationship, then that should be enough for them to rule in your favor."

Brody's head snapped up. "Um, what? We're not—"

Zya squeezed his hand hard and said, "Does it matter that we haven't been together that long? We just, um… got together when Brody moved to town. But we've been best friends for years and have known each other forever."

Brody turned to stare at her with wide eyes.

Zya gave him a just-go-with-it look.

Lorna glanced between them, her eyes narrowing before they focused on Brody. "You are together, aren't you?"

"Yes," Zya said, willing Brody to go along with the story. If this was what it took to make sure that he kept custody of his daughter, then she was all in. She'd do anything for him. She just hoped he knew that.

"Brody?" Lorna asked him, clearly skeptical. "Just be honest with me. I am most effective when I know the whole truth."

A wave of unease swept over Zya, but it quickly vanished when she imagined Winnie living with Brody's parents. Her life wouldn't be anything like the one Brody was building for her in Keating Hollow. She'd be brought up by a team of caregivers and sent to private schools. On paper, she'd have a top-notch education and everything she ever needed. Except for love. Brody's parents would only see Winnie as a reflection of themselves. There wouldn't be any golf cart rides, walks in the woods, funny faces on her pancakes, or tea parties with her favorite stuffed animals and her father. Zya just couldn't let that happen.

Brody had been staring at Zya. When their gazes met, he gave her a slow nod as if he'd just been reading her mind. Then he took a deep breath and kissed the back of Zya's hand. "Yes, it's true. We're together. Winnie already loves Zya, and we're making a life together here in Keating Hollow."

"Okay then," Lorna said with a swift nod. "That will be good for our case. Now let's go over your child care plans, where you'll live, and your finances. All of that will shape how we create our argument."

Oh crap. Zya wanted to kick herself. It was one thing to claim that they were together, to act like a couple for the judge. It was entirely another to lie about where they'd live. Although, Brody's place wouldn't be ready to live in for months. As far as anyone knew, she and Brody did live together. And that wouldn't be changing anytime soon.

"Okay," Brody said, blowing out a breath. "We live at Zya's house. Winnie started preschool and for now, she's in daycare at the school until I get off work, which is fairly flexible, so I can often pick her up when school is finished. And I'll get you copies of what? My bank statements? W-2s?"

Zya sat back in her chair as the two went back and forth about what the lawyer would need. Eventually, Brody told her about the property he was buying, but he kept it vague by just mentioning he wanted to open a hobby winery.

About an hour later, the lawyer looked at Zya and asked, "What is your roll in Winnie's upbringing? Do you have a roll, or are you just Brody's partner?"

Taken aback, Zya sat up straight and stared the attorney down. She didn't know why the question offended her, but it did. The idea that she wouldn't have a place in Winnie's life other than her relationship with the child's father made her bristle. "Of course I'm involved in her upbringing. I share a house with them, don't I? Winnie is important to me. I spend as much time with her as I do her father."

The lawyer seemed unfazed by Zya's sharp tone. "Do you watch her when Brody isn't around? Do you drop her off or pick her up from school? Do you discipline her?"

"Yes. She does those things," Brody said. "When I need her to, she does them."

It wasn't the complete truth. So far, Brody had been careful to not take advantage of Zya's time by asking her to watch Winnie. But he had to know that Zya *would* do any of those things if asked. There was no question. Zya loved that little girl. She'd do anything to help out.

Lorna nodded. "All right. I think this is enough for now. I'll let you know when the court date is set."

"What about my parents?" Brody asked.

"What about them?" Lorna tilted her head to the side, waiting.

"My mother keeps calling me. I haven't answered. Should I resume contact or not?"

Lorna clasped her hands together and placed them on her desk as she leaned forward. "Honestly, Brody, it's best if you don't talk to them. Anything you say or do that gives them a glimpse into your life here could be used as ammunition, even if you think it's harmless. From a legal standpoint, I advise you to keep your distance. However, this is family we're talking about, and I understand that they are your parents. Whatever you decide to do, just keep me in the loop."

Brody's face hardened. "They aren't my parents. Not anymore. Not after this. There will be no contact unless they ambush me."

The lawyer gave him a swift nod and said, "Okay then. I'll be in touch."

"Let's go," Brody said, placing his hand on the small of Zya's back.

Zya knew he was putting on a show for the lawyer, but she couldn't deny just how much she liked having him touch her as if they really were a couple. It was the familiarity of it that made her want to live in the moment forever.

They didn't speak until they'd climbed into Brody's truck.

He sat in the driver's seat, his hands clutching the wheel, but he made no effort to start the vehicle.

"Brody, I…" She trailed off, not at all sure what to say.

He slowly turned his head in her direction. "You what? Lied to my lawyer so that it would help my case?"

"Well, yes." Zya placed her hands in her lap to keep from fidgeting. It wasn't like her to be anxious, and this was no time to start. "I know I sprung that on you, and I shouldn't have. Not like that. But I'm not sorry. If it helps you keep custody of Winnie, then I'll pretend to be your girlfriend for as long as it takes."

"Pretend," he said softly, not looking at her, and then he shook his head as he started the truck.

"Brody?" she asked, frowning at him. "If you're not sure about this, we can go in and tell your lawyer the truth."

He cut his gaze to her. "Is that what you want to do?"

"No," she said automatically. "I want to make sure your parents don't get away with this crap. If that means I need to play your girlfriend, then that's what I'll do. You know I love that little girl. I'd do anything for her."

She'd do anything for Brody, too, but she was afraid if she said it at that moment he'd see right through her. He'd know that she'd always wanted him. The last thing she needed was for him to think she was doing this because she hoped to make it a reality. Zya would never try to do that to him. All she wanted was what was best for both him and Winnie.

That meant he could not lose his daughter to his heartless parents.

"Then from now on, as far as everyone else is concerned, you're mine, Zya Rossi. No more dates with Charles or anyone else. Got it?"

Zya let out a bark of laughter. "Dating Charles was never a possibility anyway."

"Good." He pulled out of the parking space and headed toward downtown. "Then if you don't need to get right back to work, I'm taking my girlfriend to lunch before it's time to pick Winnie up from school."

"Lunch it is," Zya said, unable to help the small smile that claimed her lips.

CHAPTER 11

*B*rody clutched Zya's hand, desperate to never let it go. What she'd done for him back at the lawyer's office still had him reeling. He'd been shocked when she'd announced that they were dating. And then his gut had twisted and it had become crystal clear that he wanted her to be his.

Now he just had to figure out how to make that a reality.

Brody tugged on the door of the Keating Hollow Brewery and held it open for Zya. "After you."

She smiled and slipped past him, but before she could slip her hand from his, he quickly followed, tightening his grip. As they stood at the hostess stand, she glanced down at their connected hands and then raised an eyebrow at him. "Am I ever going to get that back?"

"Nope."

The hostess arrived and guided them to a booth. It wasn't until she slid into the seat across from him that he reluctantly let go of her.

Zya eyed her hand and then smirked at him. "That didn't last long."

"Don't worry, Zy. There's plenty of handholding in your near future." He winked at her and then grinned when her cheeks flushed a light pink. He couldn't remember the last time he'd gotten that type of response from her. Not since they'd been teenagers.

"Well, okay then." She ducked her head behind the menu.

He chuckled.

"Stop," she ordered, but there wasn't any heat behind the word.

"I don't think I will," he said, enjoying this more than he should. "You wanted to be my girlfriend, and now you're going to find out exactly what that's like."

The menu dropped to the table, and Zya stared at him, her eyes wide. "Exactly what that's like? Just what kind of girl do you think I am, Brody Saxon? I said I'd *pretend* to be your girlfriend. I never said I wanted *to be* your girlfriend. Big distinction there."

"That's not what I heard," he teased, loving that he was making her squirm a little. It was nice to have something besides the custody case to focus on. The past two days had been pure hell. After being served the custody papers, he'd vacillated between pure rage and feeling completely wounded. He'd honestly wondered if he'd ever feel anything else. Now here he was, able to joke and flirt with Zya, all because she'd been willing to do anything to help him. "You said you were my girlfriend, so I'm just going with that."

Zya rolled her eyes. "I hope you aren't expecting conjugal visits, because that might be taking things too far."

"If I'm not allowed to date anyone else while this is going on, then…"

"Brody!"

He tossed his head back and laughed, feeling almost normal for the first time in days.

"You're impossible," Zya said, covering her eyes with her hand.

"I'm just trying to make the most of the situation," he said and then gently pulled her hand from her face. "Hey. You know I'm not serious, right?"

"For a minute there, I wasn't sure."

Honestly, he wasn't either. At that moment, nothing sounded better to him than wrapping his arms around her and kissing her until they both wondered why they'd waited so long. But Zya was his best friend, and there were reasons he'd never made a move on her before. Reasons that hadn't changed. The most important one for him and his daughter was that while Zya was the most loyal friend he'd ever had, she wasn't so great at commitment when it came to the men in her life. Not that Brody had any room to judge her. He'd only had one serious relationship as well as a series of meaningless hookups. Meanwhile, she'd had a few long-term relationships, but the ones that had lasted had ended with Zya bolting. Like when she left Carter. She hadn't just left *him*, she'd left home and moved to a small town across the country so she didn't have to deal with any of it. They were a disaster waiting to happen, right?

But what if they weren't? What if the reason they'd never had a successful relationship last was because they were meant to be together?

What if Brody got close to Zya romantically and it didn't work out? Would she bolt then, too? Would he? He just couldn't take the risk. Not when he had Winnie to consider. And not when he was battling his parents for custody.

Brody reached across the table and covered Zya's hand.

"We're friends, Zy. Always have been and always will be. You know that, right?"

She glanced down at his hand, swallowed, and then nodded. "Yes."

"Thank you for... everything. Opening your home to us, helping me with Winnie, and for being willing to pretend to date me at least until we can get this case dismissed."

"I'd do anything for you, Brody. You have to know that." She turned her hand over and slipped her fingers between his, holding on tightly.

His eyes burned with unexpected tears and he quickly blinked them back as he choked out, "Thanks."

"There's no need to thank me," she said softly. "I love you and Winnie. This is what friends do."

No it wasn't. Friends didn't put themselves in the middle of someone else's legal battle. Usually they remained supportive. They offered lawyer referrals or were willing to write a character statement. But to pretend to be a significant other for weeks, if not months, was on a whole other level. But this was Zya. His Zya. Their friendship was something special. "I love you, too, Zy."

While caressing the back of his hand with her thumb, she said, "Okay then. No more thanking me, got it?"

"Got it." He gave her a sharp nod and tried not to think about the tingles she was creating with her gentle touch. It was so innocent. And yet, if she didn't stop, he really was going to lose his mind.

"Sorry about that! I had a large party I was handling. I didn't mean to make you wait so long." A waitress with a long black ponytail whipped out an order pad and asked, "What can I get you?"

Brody ordered a burger, fries, and a large apple cider.

"I'll have the same," Zya said, handing her menu to the waitress.

"I'm on it. Be right back with those drinks." The waitress hurried away, and Brody gaped at Zya.

"What?" she asked, patting her face as if she were trying to find a smudge of something to wipe off. "Why are you looking at me like that?"

"Like what?" he asked, amused again.

"Like I have ketchup smeared all over my face."

"Oh, that." He chuckled. "I guess I'm just surprised by your order. A burger and fries? I haven't seen you eat fries since... I don't know. Junior year in college?"

"There's no harm in splurging every now and then," she said with a sniff.

"No argument from me," he said. Then he sat back in the booth and let out a long sigh.

Zya studied him, giving him a sympathetic look. "Want to talk about it?"

Brody appreciated that his friend could change gears so suddenly. He'd been teasing and flirting with her ever since they'd arrived at the restaurant. But she hadn't forgotten why they were together in the middle of the day on a Tuesday when they were both normally at work. Zya had closed her store so that she could be with him and lend her support. She'd never know how much that meant to him.

"What is there to say?" he asked her. "My parents are even worse than I thought. I don't think I'll ever be able to forgive them for this."

"I know, Brody. Me neither." She shook her head. "I just don't understand why they're doing this. It doesn't make sense to me. They don't seem like the kind of people who are particularly interested in childrearing. I mean, they let the nannies raise you, didn't they?"

"They did," he confirmed with a grimace. "But it's not about raising Winnie. It's about me. Or, to be more precise, it's about controlling me."

Zya scowled. "They think that by threatening to take your daughter away, that you'll fall in line and go to work for your father?"

"Maybe." Brody pressed his fingertips to his temple as he continued. "When I moved to France, they nearly lost their minds. Dad tried to bribe me with everything he could think of to get me to stay in Salem. You remember that, right?"

"Sure," she said with a nod. "They were ready to buy you a house, a fancy car, and…" She raised her eyebrows nearly to the top of her hairline. "I think you even mentioned that your dad said something about a mail order bride?"

Brody let out a humorless chuckle. "Yeah, I might have exaggerated that part, but had I requested one, I'm certain I'd be married to a Natalya by now."

"That's disturbing."

"Tell me about it." Brody picked up his fork and started fiddling with it. "When I said no to all their offers, next came the threats. Things like writing me out of the will and cutting off my access to the beach house in Rhode Island and the ski cabin in Vermont."

Zya grimaced and something dark flickered in her eyes. "They cut you off just because you moved to France for a job?"

"And Colette. Don't forget her. They didn't approve. They never said why they hated her so much, but I can guess it's because she didn't have the right background or the right connections with the powerful elite in France. If she had, they'd have seen her as an asset and would've worked hard to get into her good graces. Instead, they shunned her and did everything in their power to keep me home. When it didn't work, they blamed her. Hell, they even blamed her for Winnie's existence. It's disgusting."

"How on earth is it Colette's fault that you knocked up a one-night stand?" Zya demanded.

"Because she didn't keep her man happy. Obviously." The disgust in Brody's tone was unmistakable.

"What in the actual hell?" Zya said, her voice low and full of incredulity. "It's her fault you were out there knocking up some random girl? Talk about toxic. Your parents are the worst."

"I certainly think so. The only reason they are trying to get Winnie is that they see her as a way to control their only son, who wants nothing to do with the family business or his manipulative parents. They think if they win this I'll go running back to Salem and will take a job with my father because they know I'll do anything for Winnie."

"Would you?" Zya asked, pressing her hand to her throat.

Brody let out a snarl as he said, "Go back and work for that vile man? Yeah, I would if I had to. If they win custody and it's the only way to see my daughter, I'll spend the next fifteen years doing whatever it takes to be in her life. I won't be a missing father again, Zy. I can't. I won't."

She nodded. "I know. You'd do what you had to. Your heart is just too big not to."

His heart would be shattered if he lost Winnie. There was no choice when it came to his daughter. "We just have to win this case. That's all there is to it."

Zya slipped out of her side of the booth and slid in beside Brody. She wrapped her arms around him, hugging him tightly against her. Brody gladly melted into her, holding on for dear life.

"You mean the world to me, Zya. Like family. My only family," he said softly.

"Not *like* family, Brody. We *are* family. And don't you ever forget it." She pressed her lips to his cheek, giving him a gentle kiss that made him instinctively turn to her.

Their lips were a mere inch apart. The air between them crackled with a current of electricity, and Brody couldn't help but stare at her sweet mouth. When her tongue darted out, wetting her lips, he nearly groaned. There was no thought. No planning. Nothing other than sheer instinct.

He couldn't keep himself from her any longer. She was just too tempting.

Brody cupped her cheek with one palm and then lifted her chin with his thumb, stroking the delicate skin of her neck.

Zya's green eyes bore into his, holding his intense gaze.

There was no denying the connection between them. It was raw and powerful, and he was starting to feel like he'd die if he didn't kiss her.

"Dammit, Zy. This is a bad idea," he said softly, just before he covered her lips with his own.

Zya let out a soft moan that made his entire body shiver with desire. Their lips were barely touching, but it was the most powerful kiss he'd ever shared with a woman. With just the barely there kiss, he felt her everywhere and knew in that one moment that she was meant to be his. They weren't just friends. They were so much more.

He wrapped his arms around her, pulling her in closer, and was just about to take the plunge and deepen the kiss when he heard the plunk of two glasses hitting the table.

Zya jerked back suddenly, looking dazed and more than a

little rattled. "What... I mean, how..." She cleared her throat. "That was—"

"Just one kiss, Zya," Brody said patiently. "Now the entire town will know." He nodded toward Ms. Betty, who was sitting a few tables away. She had her phone pointed in their direction, and he had the distinct feeling that the older woman had been filming them.

"Don't stop on my account!" Ms. Betty called from her table. "You have no idea how much those horny women down at the retirement village will pay for footage like this."

Zya blinked at her. "Footage of a barely there kiss?"

"It's not the act, sweetheart. It's the heat behind it," Ms. Betty explained. "And, honey, that was hot." The older woman fanned herself widely with one hand before she got up, grabbed her bag, and rushed off, apparently to sell the video of Brody kissing Zya.

"Well, if we wanted people to think we're a couple, I think we just succeeded," Zya said, scooting off the bench and hurrying back over to her side.

"I think you're right." Brody lifted his cider glass and held it up for a toast.

Zya did the same and touched his glass lightly. "What are we toasting to?"

Brody gave her a cocky grin and said, "To us. No matter what happens, I know that with you by my side, it's going to be a wild ride."

"To the wild ride," Zya said, her eyes sparkling with determination.

Brody clinked his glass to hers and knew no truer words had ever been spoken.

CHAPTER 12

Zya woke before dawn. She lay staring at her ceiling, her mind fully alert, while her body begged her to stay snuggled in her bed. But when she felt her skin start to tingle as if a spirit was trying to make itself known to her, she knew she could no longer put off her usual walk in the woods.

Ever since Brody had arrived, her routine had been off. She had only taken a few walks, and none of them had been down to the lagoon. Today she had no choice. It was time to strengthen her wards. Otherwise, her aunts would be back to torment her with more blind dates.

As she swung her legs out of her bed, her cat Lyra slinked over and climbed into her lap, rubbing her head against Zya's stomach.

"Morning, sweet pea," Zya said, running her hand down her fur baby's back.

Lyra started to purr and tried to curl up right there on Zya.

"Sorry, girl. It's time for Mama to get up." Zya gently lifted her cat and placed her next to her pillow. "Get some more sleep. Brody will feed you when he gets up."

Her cat gave her a forlorn look but didn't move as Zya disappeared into her bathroom to get ready to start her day.

Twenty minutes later, Zya was dressed in her workout pants and a sweatshirt and ready to start her morning. She moved silently down the hall, not wanting to wake either Brody or Winnie. They wouldn't get up for another hour or so. When she reached Brody's room, she was somewhat surprised to see the door open. She wasn't going to peek in, but when Lyra slipped past her into the room, she went after her cat, only to stop when she spotted Winnie curled up on Brody's chest, the two of them sound asleep.

They didn't even move when Lyra jumped up onto the bed and curled up next to Brody.

Zya clutched at her heart as she took in the scene. Gods, she loved them. All three of them. A vision of Zya, Brody, and Winnie, all cuddled up together in that bed flashed in her mind, and the desire to climb in beside them was almost too much to resist.

Almost.

She quickly back-pedaled and hurried out of the room, her heart aching. It was becoming harder and harder to deny that she'd fallen head over heels for her best friend and his delightful daughter.

"Stop," Zya whispered to herself. It would do her no good to keep fantasizing about a life that would never be hers. It was one thing to pretend to be dating Brody to help him with the custody case. It was entirely another to act as if that could be a reality. It would only end up hurting her in the end. Even if there was something more than friendship between them, she didn't think either of them would act on it. That would be too risky. Brody was the most important person in her life, and if she lost him… She shook her head. It was too painful to even think about.

Zya stopped in the kitchen for a sip of water and then silently slipped out the back door. The morning mist was cool on her face as she made her way through the woods. The sounds of breaking twigs from her footsteps and the brush of foliage against her jacket filled the silence. She slipped out from between the trees and just ahead, she spotted the pure white wolf waiting patiently for her just as he always did first thing in the morning.

"Hey, Silver," she said and held out her hand to the majestic creature.

He pushed his head into her open palm, inviting her to pet him. She scratched behind his ears. After a few moments, he shook his head and started to trot forward, taking her along their path that wound its way through the woods and to a lagoon that was on the east side of Wanda and Cam's property. It was her preferred place to cast her spells as water was a magical conductor for her.

Not long after Zya had moved to town, she'd been down at the lagoon when she'd run into Wanda, and Wanda had given her permission to use the lagoon whenever she wanted. It wasn't near Wanda and Cam's new house, so it appeared they didn't visit the area often. In fact, Zya hadn't seen Wanda there at any other time than that day, and she was a frequent visitor.

The closer Zya got to the lagoon, the more she felt the faint buzz of magic that emanated from the area. Her own magic answered the call and pooled at her fingertips, ready to be unleashed.

Silver paused, his ears twitching.

"What is it, boy?" she asked softly.

The wolf was standing stock-still, and then suddenly he took off at full speed, headed straight for the lagoon.

A shiver ran up Zya's spine, but she steeled herself and pushed forward. Something was calling to her, but she could hear her mother's voice in her head. *Zya, your curiosity is going to get the best of you one of these days. When are you going to learn to not run head first into trouble?*

When it came to magic and her powers, Zya was never one to turn away. All of it fascinated her too much. Besides, with Silver by her side, she had a fierce protector. Determined to see what had set off the wolf, Zya followed his path.

The trees gave way to the lagoon, and Zya knew immediately what had drawn the wolf. A ghost in a long trench coat stood at the water's edge, his presence soaking up all the magic that usually crackled in the air. There was no use trying to put up her walls now. She'd use far too much energy. She had to wait until this ghost moved on. Then she'd use the lagoon to do what she needed to do.

The wolf was just ahead, watching and waiting.

Zya stepped up beside the wolf and said, "What do you want?"

The ghost slowly turned around.

"Grandfather?" Zya asked, pressing her hand to her chest. "Is that really you?" She was used to her aunts visiting her, but the last time she'd seen her grandfather, he'd been walking out the door, headed to the market. He'd collapsed in the parking lot from a blood clot.

"Zya," he said with a slow nod. "It's good to see you, child."

She wanted to run to him and hug him, but she knew that wasn't possible. She could see and talk to ghosts, but that didn't make them solid beings. Still, she couldn't help raising her arm as if she were reaching out to him. When she noticed what she was doing, she dropped it to her side and said, "I've missed you."

"I know, Zya. But we both know this is the way of life. Let's just enjoy this moment while we can." He waved for her to join him near the water.

She hurried to his side, but Silver stayed rooted where he was near the tree line.

Her grandfather didn't seem to be in a hurry to speak, and Zya was happy to take in the moment, to just be near him again. It was one of those times when she knew she just had to be present. To enjoy every moment she had with him. Because if he hadn't shown up until now, then it wasn't likely he'd show up again in the near future. Not unless it was for something important.

"You've done well for yourself, child," he said, smiling down at her warmly.

"Mom doesn't approve."

He snorted. "Yes, she does. She's just having trouble letting go."

Zya raised one eyebrow.

This time he smirked. "Your mother is a complicated woman, but she loves you. She only wants the best for you."

"Her best for me is to stay and marry a cheater who only cares about himself," Zya said flatly.

"Her advice might be a little misguided." His words were gentle, and Zya felt like they were wrapping around her like a hug.

"This isn't what you came here to tell me, is it?"

"No. It's not. But it's been a long time. Can't I just enjoy a moment with my granddaughter?"

She turned to look up at him, finding his expression full of love. "Yes. Yes, you can. I'll stand here all day and all night if you want me to, Gramps."

"You and I both know I don't have that much time."

It was true. Ghosts could usually only stick around for a short time before they burned their energy out. It was probably why he'd chosen to meet her at the lagoon. The power that was steeped into the area would help him maintain his energy for longer than if he just popped into her shop or even her house.

"Troubling times are ahead, Zya," he said quietly.

"You mean with Brody?" she asked as an ache formed in her gut.

"Yes and no."

"That's awfully vague," she said.

"I know. I don't mean to be. Not everything is clear even to me."

"Can you tell me which direction the trouble is coming from?" she asked.

"All sides, Zya. All of them."

She groaned. "What am I supposed to do with that?"

"Just be ready for the coming fight. And, Zya?"

"Yeah?" Her grandfather's image was starting to fade, and Zya knew their time was limited.

"Always fight for those you love. That's what's most important. Understand?"

Before she could answer, he was gone.

"Kitty!" Winnie's high-pitched, excitable voice carried through the window as Zya approached the house.

Zya had been lost in thought after her grandfather's visit

and hadn't even realized she was almost back to the house. After her grandfather had disappeared, she'd abandoned the idea of setting her wards against spirits. She couldn't take that risk in case her grandfather wanted to pay her another visit. Instead, she'd turned around and headed back into the woods where she moved on autopilot.

Just as Zya reached for her back door, she turned and spotted the white wolf standing at the tree line. His amber gaze bore into hers before he trotted back into the woods.

"See you tomorrow, friend," she said softly and then walked into the house.

"Zya's home!" Winnie called from her spot at the table.

"Hey, sweetie pie." Zya hurried over to her and gave the little girl a kiss on her head. "Did you sleep well?"

"I slept with Daddy." She grinned and pointed at Lyra. "And your kitty."

"I saw that this morning. You wanna know a secret?"

She nodded vigorously.

"I was a little jealous. You looked so cozy all curled up like a bug in a rug."

Winnie bounced in her chair, kicking her legs as she laughed.

Zya glanced up at Brody. "Good morning."

He gave her an inquisitive look. "Jealous, huh?"

"Can you blame me? You were cuddled up with my favorite girl and my cat. That looked a lot better than a predawn hike." She winked at him.

"For future reference, there's always room for more cuddling." Brody placed an omelet in front of her and said, "Sit. Breakfast is ready."

Zya took her place at the table, loving her new reality. Every morning that she'd gone out for her walks with the wolf,

Brody was there with breakfast waiting for her when she got back home. Before he'd moved in, her breakfasts were usually a piece of toast or a yogurt. Now she was getting the full-service treatment, and it just made her feel appreciated… and loved. "Thank you."

"Of course." He handed her a mug of coffee and then sat across from her.

Breakfast was lively these days, usually with a running commentary from Winnie as she chatted about anything and everything. This morning it was all about Lyra and how she wanted to take the cat to school with her. Brody was good at deflecting though, and soon enough, the little girl had moved on to talking about PJ, her favorite stuffed animal.

Zya decided her grandfather knew what he was talking about. Fighting for the people who were sitting at her table really was the most important thing. Without them, nothing else really mattered.

When they were done eating, Zya cleared the table and went to work on loading the dishwasher while Brody helped Winnie finish getting ready for school. Just as Zya was finishing up, Brody came back in the kitchen and stood behind her with his hands kneading her shoulders.

"That's amazing," Zya said with a groan.

"Thanks for cleaning up."

She let out a huff of laughter. "Thank you for cooking breakfast. I'm starting to feel really spoiled, you know. A girl could get used to this."

Brody let out his own soft laugh before he leaned in, kissed her on the cheek, and said, "Good."

Then he was gone, leaving her stunned with her cheek tingling. She was still just standing there like a complete idiot when Winnie came running in a moment later and said, "I wanna go with you, Zya."

"To work?" she asked, startled as she turned the water off.

"She wants you to take her to school," Brody said from the kitchen doorway. He was holding her backpack in one hand while reaching out to Winnie. "Zya has to go to work, Winnie. Come on. I'll take you."

"I can do it," Zya said quickly. "Besides, the school is on my way. It's not a big deal." She hurried off to her room to get cleaned up and ready for her day, and when she returned, she found them waiting for her in the living room.

"Ready, sweetie pie?" Zya asked Winnie.

Winnie jumped up from the couch, taking her small backpack from her dad, and then ran to Zya's side.

Brody shook his head, smiling at them. "I know when I've been outvoted. Okay, fine. You two go on ahead. Winnie, I'll pick you up after work."

His daughter gave him a halfhearted wave and stared up at Zya. "Can the kitty come, too?"

"Not this time, cutie pie. Lyra's planning on guarding the house today," Zya said, taking Winnie's hand. "Let's get moving before we're both late."

"Okay." Winnie ran over to Lyra, who was sitting in a cat bed in the corner, patted her head and said, "Be good, kitty."

Lyra gave Winnie the side-eye and then slinked off into the hallway toward Zya's bedroom where she wouldn't be bothered by any of them.

Zya stifled a chuckle, took Winnie by the hand, and led the little girl out to her Jeep, where she buckled her into the new car seat that Brody had gotten for her. He'd said it was so that is was believable to say that Zya actually did help with pickups and drop offs at school. But Zya was prepared to make full use of the new seat, because as far as she was concerned, she'd spend as much time with Winnie as she could. In just a handful of days, Zya had fallen completely in love with the little girl. And it wasn't only because she belonged to Brody. No, it was because she was pure joy, and Zya considered herself lucky to have even a tiny place in her life. As long as she was allowed to, she'd take the little girl where ever she needed to go. Her yarn shop would just have to wait.

CHAPTER 13

"*H*ey, hey, if it isn't TikTok's newest celebrity," Candy Pelsh called out as she entered Brody's office. The young woman, who looked to be in her early twenties, was wearing faded jeans and a stylish white sweater that was a nice contrast to her dark skin. She was his boss's niece and sometimes helped out at the winery when they needed a pair of extra hands.

Brody jerked his head up from the spreadsheet he'd been studying. He was sitting behind his desk in his office that was located in the corner of the Pelsh wine cellar. It was an interesting place to put the vintner since it never got above sixty-five degrees. But Brody preferred to be with the wine rather than in an office somewhere else on the grounds.

He'd learned early on that he had a special connection to the grapes. His earth witch magic really came alive when he was near the grapes. And for him, it was like a sixth sense when he knew the wine was done aging. If his office wasn't in the cellar, he might miss the optimal time to bottle the next season's inventory.

"I'm not even on TikTok," Brody said without pulling his attention from his Excel sheets. "You must be mistaken."

"Oh, I'm very much not mistaken," she said with a giggle as she pulled out her phone. "Look at this." After tapping a couple of times on her screen, she turned it around so he could see the video.

It was a little off center, but it was definitely him. And Zya. It was the video that Ms. Betty had taken of him kissing Zya at the brewery the day before. His gaze was glued to Zya and her body language. Her eyes were closed and her head was tilted just so that the curve of her neck was nothing less than tantalizing. Why hadn't he run his hand down her smooth skin? That had definitely been a missed opportunity, and his fingers twitched with the desire to touch her again.

"It's been up for less than twenty-four hours, and it already has over a million streams," Candy said. "And because it's so hot, memes are popping up everywhere."

"What?" Brody asked, snapping out of his hazy fog. "It's gone viral? Why?"

Candy chuckled. "Oh, you poor thing. It must be hard to be so old that you don't even understand the internet."

Brody rolled his eyes. "I understand the internet. It's just that I've never had much patience for social media. Why in the world would this video of me and Zya go viral? It's just a kiss, and it doesn't even last that long."

"Uh, because it's hot?" Candy shook her head at him. "You don't understand what turns women on at all, do you?"

Now that offended him. he'd never had trouble in that department. He sniffed, acting insulted. "I haven't had any complaints."

She snorted. "Is that some commentary on your sexual prowess? Because that's not at all the same thing as

116

understanding what's happening here." She shook the phone at him. "This is desire porn. That look on your face and the way Zya is eating it up is swoonworthy, Brody. You two want each other. It's the sexual tension that's radiating from this video that is making women claim they've gotten pregnant just by watching it."

"But it's just a kiss," he said, feeling his face flush.

"Oh, it's a lot more than that, my friend. Look here." She tapped a few more times on the screen before showing him a collection of screenshots. "You and Zya are an internet sensation."

Brody took the phone and squinted at the screenshot of him and Zya, their lips barely touching. The caption read: *How to make babies just from kissing.*

The meme actually made him a little hot under the collar. He'd read variations on that phrase more times than he could count, but it struck him differently when he was the one pictured in the meme with his best friend.

"There's more. Keep scrolling," Candy insisted.

Brody immediately swiped left.

The slower the kiss, the faster the heartbeat.

The one after that made him raise his eyebrows. *When your mountain man brings the sexy back.* "Mountain man? Where do they see that?" Brody asked Candy.

She cackled and then smirked. "It's your flannel shirt, my man. Very lumberjack and mountain mannish. They think it's sexy. Especially with your sleeves rolled up a bit. You should probably wear them more."

"Uh, okay. I didn't realize that was a thing." He continued to swipe and paused when he read, *When friends finally give in to the passion and become lovers.*

When Brody kept staring at the screen, Candy leaned over

to check out what he was looking at. Then she said, "Yeah. Looks like you have a decision to make, huh?"

He wanted to pretend he didn't know what she was talking about, but there really was no point in denying the attraction sparking between him and Zya. Hell, it was all over the internet for the entire world to see.

"Candy?" Walter Pelsh said as he walked into the cellar. The large dark-skinned man had an easy smile and a gentle personality that made him one of the best bosses that Brody had ever had. "Your aunt could use your help up at the barn. We need to finish setting up the tables for that corporate event that's happening tomorrow."

"I'm on it," she said as she took her phone out of Brody's hand. On her way out, she kissed Walter on the cheek. "Don't forget that Hanna and Rhys are coming for dinner at six."

A grin spread over Walter's face. "I'll be done by then. Thanks for the reminder, Candy."

She gave him a mock salute and then disappeared up the stairs.

Walter turned to Brody. "Candy tells me you're famous now."

"More like infamous," Brody muttered, wanting to avoid this conversation like the plague. "It's just silly internet stuff. What's up?"

Walter walked over to Brody's desk and took a seat across from him. "I wanted to take a moment to find out how it's going. If you've settled in. How you feel about working here. And last, your overall general impression of our operations. Better or worse than what you're used to? Do you see areas where we can improve? Let me have it. I want to know what's going on in that brain of yours."

"Wow. Okay," Brody said, just to get his bearings. With the

custody case, he'd had a lot of other things on his mind lately. "Well, first off, it's going well. I like working here. Considering I'm still settling in to Keating Hollow, it's nice that it's not a huge operation yet, though once I have my feet under me, I'd love to help you expand like we talked about in my interview. It's a challenge I know I'd enjoy."

"That's good," the older man said with a nod. "Because I've decided to plant more grapes next month and come harvest season this year, we'll have 25% more production than last year. Do you think you can manage that?"

"Absolutely," Brody said automatically. "I'm up for the challenge."

"Good deal." Walter sat back in his chair and eyed Brody. "Now, tell me everything you'd do differently if you owned this winery."

Brody blew out a breath. "Way to put a guy on the spot," he said with a nervous chuckle.

Walter's easy smile vanished as he leaned forward and rested his elbows on his knees. "It's not a test, Brody. I really want to know what you think. If there are better or more efficient ways to do things, I want to know about it. You know we're a fairly young winery, and I want to make sure this place not only survives, but thrives for generations to come."

That statement right there was why Brody had come to work for Walter Pelsh. The man had come across as smart, hardworking, and sincere. There hadn't been a trace of ego, unlike so many other winery owners he'd worked for. Walter Pelsh was a man who wanted to hear differing opinions. He wanted his employees to challenge him. He saw it as one of the best ways to innovate. Well, if Walter wanted his opinion, he was going to get it.

"Honestly, this is one of the best places I've ever worked,"

Brody said. "Your family's pride in the winery shows with everything you do. If I could give you one piece of advice, it'd be to not promise your wine until it's done aging."

Walter frowned. "You're telling me not to take orders until the wine is bottled?"

"That's exactly what I'm saying." Brody stood and started to pace the office. "I understand the inclination to accept preorders. The winery depends on those contracts for future income and cash flow. I get that. But what that does is put pressure on the vintner to make the call to bottle the wine as soon as possible and then it's sold at the set price."

"Yes, that's true, but establishments want to lock-in prices early so they can protect their bottom line, too. I think it's too risky not to take preorders. We might find ourselves buried in cases of wine that we can't move because distributors are already contracted with other wineries."

Brody nodded. "Yes, it's a risk. But you also miss out on special reserve wines and having the luxury of waiting until the wine is at peak flavor. To be honest, Walter, I think your wines could be international award winners if we just had the gift of patience. If we could wait just a little longer before bottling, I think the Pelsh winery will end up with an unrivaled reputation for outstanding wines."

Interest sparked in Walter's eyes. "I really like where this is going. How about we work out a compromise? I'll hold 30% of the inventory for you to do as you see fit, and I'll get contracts for the rest. If your small production shows promise this fall, we'll allocate more of the grapes your way next season."

Brody did a mental calculation and then nodded slowly. He wasn't afraid of proving himself. He'd done it before and he'd do it again. "Yes. I'd love to try that."

They spent the next hour running through ideas and

scenarios until they had the details worked out. Once they were done, Walter relaxed and propped one ankle on his knee. "Now, tell me about that property you're trying to buy. How's that going?"

The change of topic startled Brody. Ever since the news of the custody suit, he hadn't really thought about the house he was buying. Wanda had hooked him up with a great mortgage officer and since he'd sent in his information, everything had been running smoothly and according to schedule. "Good. Uh, I think I'm supposed to close in a few weeks. Once that's done, I'll start putting a plan together. This first year, I'll start small to see how things go and then I'll expand next year."

Walter nodded his approval. "Good man. If you get anything decent your first year, I'm happy to help market it to our business partners. And you can offer tastings here."

"That's..." Brody swallowed, a little overcome with emotion. "That's really generous, Walter. Thank you."

"It's just what we do for family, son. That's all." Walter stood as if he was going to leave, but then he paused and turned back. "One more thing."

"Yes?"

"Candy showed me that video of you and Zya. Looks like you've found something good there."

"Oh, that. I..." Brody shook his head, stopping himself from admitting that they weren't really a couple. He desperately didn't want to lie to his boss, but at the same time, he needed everyone in town to believe that they were together. If his parents' lawyer found out it wasn't true, the results could be devastating. "That's new."

"New or not, there's not really anything better than spending your life with your best friend, is there?" he asked, giving Brody a knowing smile. "Mary and I were friends first all those years ago before we started dating. She was my best friend then, and she's my best friend now. If you ask me, the best decision I ever made was to put aside my fears and finally let that woman know just how much I wanted her. From that day forward, we were inseparable. I hope it's the same for you and Zya."

Brody swallowed the lump in his throat. "I hope so, too."

"Are you giving love advice again, Walter?" Mary Pelsh asked as she rounded the corner and appeared in front of Brody's door.

"Again? When do I give dating advice?" he asked.

"All the time. You were just telling Candy who she should date last night at dinner." She glanced past her husband. "Hello, Brody. I hope he hasn't overstepped."

"No. Not at all," Brody said with a laugh. "On the contrary. He's been… inspirational."

"Well, he's really good at that," she said and placed a hand on her husband's chest. "I just came to let you know that the invoicing is done. If you need me, I'll be in the house. Thanks for sending Candy to help with the event tomorrow. Since she's there, I'm now able to get dinner started."

"Whatcha cooking?" Walter asked her.

"It's lasagna night." She kissed him on the cheek and started to retreat.

"Hey, Mary," Walter called to her.

"Yes, love?"

"You're looking a little hot. Overworked maybe? How about we take a break before you start on that dinner?" Walter asked, his tone somehow full of innuendo.

She laughed, her eyes crinkling at the edges. "Are you sure you have time for a *break*?"

"We'll make it quick," he said and hurried after her. He

hastily waved at Brody as he grabbed her around the waist and they shuffled out of the cellar, both of them laughing like teenagers.

Brody sat there listening as their laughter faded. His soul ached for what the Pelshes had together, and the feeling startled him. Was that really what he wanted? To be tied down to one person?

To Zya.

He knew the answer. It was as clear as night and day. He just had to find the courage to go for it.

CHAPTER 14

*Z*ya opened another box that carried her favorite yarn from Juniper Moon Farm and checked the packing slip to make sure she got everything she'd ordered. After a quick scan, she determined everything was there and got busy restocking her shelves.

She'd spent the morning in her shop lost in thought after her conversation with her grandfather. The message had been fairly straightforward. Trouble was coming, and she should be sure to fight for those she loved. Hadn't trouble already arrived? And hadn't she already stepped up, proving she'd fight for those she loved?

It didn't make sense that her grandfather would use all his energy to show up and deliver that message when she didn't exactly need to hear it. Ghosts didn't usually work that way. It made her wonder what she should be prepared for in the coming days.

The bells chimed on the door, and she heard a couple of women talking and laughing.

Zya poked her head out from behind a display and spotted

two of the Townsend sisters, Abby and Yvette. Abby's hair was pulled up into a bun, with tendrils of curls framing her face, while Yvette's auburn locks flowed freely. "Hey," she said. "I'll be right there." Zya grabbed the open box of yarn and carried it over behind the front counter where the sisters were waiting for her.

"Zya!" Abby said and flung her arms around her. "I'm so excited for you. Big changes, huh?"

"Changes?" Zya asked as she awkwardly hugged the pretty blonde. "What changes?"

"You know, dating Brody and suddenly having a three-year-old living in your house," Abby said. "Believe me when I say there's nothing harder than raising kids. But there's also nothing more rewarding, right?"

"Right," Zya agreed, nodding, but then she frowned slightly. "But Winnie isn't hard at all. She's one of the most easygoing kids I've ever met, and if anyone has a reason to lash out, it's her." After losing her mom and being moved to a completely different country with a man she barely knew, it was unbelievable that she'd adjusted so well. But Brody's pediatrician had told him that younger kids usually do transition easier in these situations. Sure, Winnie would always miss her mom, but her ability to adapt was impressive and apparently not completely unexpected.

"She's a sweetie for sure," Yvette said, pushing her long chestnut hair out of her eyes. Yvette was the oldest of the five Townsend sisters and the owner of the Keating Hollow bookstore, Hollow Books. She and Zya had become friendly over the past year mainly due to Brinn Taylor, one of Yvette's employees. Brinn invited Zya to pretty much every event that happened in Keating Hollow and most of them included the Townsend sisters and a handful of their friends.

"You've met her?" Zya asked, wondering when that had happened.

"She goes to the same preschool as Skye," Yvette explained. "Skye adores Winnie by the way. Do you think Brody would be interested in letting her come over for a play date?"

"I'm sure he would," Zya said, her heart elated that Winnie was making a friend.

"Ahh, preschool," Abby sighed wistfully. "What I wouldn't give for a few hours all to myself. It's a miracle I'm out now. If it wasn't for Clay having the day off, I'd be stuck on mommy duty. Sixteen-month-olds don't really appreciate it when their mommies decide they need even five minutes to themselves."

"How is your little one?" Zya asked her. "What's her name again?"

Abby beamed. "She's wonderful. And her name is Lynette, after my father."

"Abby's really pushing for that favorite-child distinction," Yvette teased. "Dad is still over the moon about her name. I swear, he acts like she's his little mini-me with the time he spends with her."

"That's really sweet," Zya said, waiting for her flight response to kick in. It usually did when the conversation focused almost exclusively on kids or childrearing responsibilities. But for some reason, today it didn't. She just kept picturing Winnie cuddled up with Brody and her cat Lyra and started to wonder why she'd always thought she'd never want kids.

"It is sweet," Yvette agreed. "My sister is also a kiss-ass."

Abby swatted Yvette playfully. "Stop. Dad deserves to be honored and you know it."

"Of course he does," Yvette agreed. "But since I'm the older sister, I'm never going to give you a break."

Zya watched the two of them in amusement. She didn't have sisters. Or any siblings for that matter. So the way the Townsend sisters interacted with each other was always fascinating to her. Zya loved the way they needled each other to get under their skin but also fiercely protected each other. She'd had something sort of like that with a cousin of hers, but the intimate familiarity just wasn't there.

"Listen, Zya," Abby said. "I'm looking for some bulky weight yarn so I can make some blankets for Faith's triplets. Something that will work up fast so I won't still be working on it when they're headed off to college."

"Triplets. Wow. How old are they?" Zya asked as she gestured for the women to follow her to the far wall.

"Just about a year old," Yvette said. "I don't know how she and Hunter do it all to be honest. I can barely remember to brush my teeth in the morning, and I only have two little ones."

"Someone just told me the other day that they're easier when they're little," Abby said with a grimace.

"You've got to be kidding!" Yvette said with a shudder. "If it's harder than this when they're teenagers, I'm gonna have to demand a do-over."

Zya laughed.

But Abby nodded sagely. "Yes, I could use a do-over after this morning's shenanigans. Can you believe that Olive came out of my room with a full face of makeup this morning? And she was wearing a skirt so short I thought she'd joined a cheerleader team."

"What did you do?" Yvette asked, unable to hide her chuckle.

"Oh, laugh now," Abby said. "In a few years when Skye is giving you attitude, I'll remind you of this."

"Skye would never," Yvette insisted.

"That's what I said about Olive," Abby said. "But she just turned thirteen, and I swear she's been swallowed whole by a demon. The night before her birthday, she was our sweet, loving little girl who liked to make s'mores with her daddy. And then the very next day, she didn't want anything to do with Clay and became obsessed with black and keeps asking for a lip piercing. And don't get me started on the smudged black eyeliner."

Zya couldn't help but laugh. "Sounds like you've got the makings of a potential goth girl on your hands."

Abby groaned. "You don't understand. Overnight she went from rainbows and unicorns to…" She waved a hand around in the air. "I don't know. The princess of darkness. And not in a cool Wednesday Adams kind of way. More like an angry Jessica Jones kind of way. I'm half expecting to find a bottle of Jack and a spell book of curses in her backpack."

"It's not even remotely that bad," Yvette said with a roll of her eyes. "Every teenager goes through their self-expression stage. You just need to wait her out."

Zya nodded in support. "I went through a black leather and thigh-high spiked boots stage when I was in high school. I even got a nose piercing. It made my mom lose her mind, and honestly, even though it wasn't conscious at the time, I'm 99% sure I only did it to get a rise out of her." She touched Abby's arm lightly. "I suggest you don't make a big deal about the changes. It's likely, once she realizes you and Clay don't really care, she'll go back to resembling someone you recognize."

"Goddess above," Abby said, looking at the ceiling, "I hope you're right."

"I hope so, too," Zya said and then excused herself when the shop phone started to ring. Zya left them with the bulky yarn and ran back to the front of the store, grabbing the phone when it was on its fourth ring. "Hello, Witches in Stitches."

"Hey, Zya."

Carter. Zya's breath caught in her throat and for a moment there, she thought her heart had stopped beating, too.

"Zy, are you still there," he asked, sounding annoyed.

"Yes, I'm still here, Carter. Why are you calling me?" Her voice was like ice, and she was proud of herself for not showing any other emotion. It wasn't that she had feelings for the man anymore. But he did have the knowledge and ability to push all her buttons.

"That's no way to greet your fiancé," he admonished.

"You're not my fiancé," she spat out, irritation churning through her limbs.

"Fine, ex-fiancé. Happy now?" he asked, keeping his tone light as if all of this was a joke. To him, it probably was.

"What do you want?" she demanded, knowing she should just hang up. But it had been more than a year since she'd talked to him, and she couldn't deny that she was curious as to why he was suddenly calling.

There was a crackle of static on the line before Carter spoke so softly she wasn't sure she'd heard him correctly. "I want you to come home."

"Come home?" she parroted, her confusion ringing loud and clear in her tone. "What home, Carter? My home is here now and it has been for over a year."

He sighed heavily as if exasperated. "You've been gone too long, Zy. Don't you think you've punished me enough? I'm sorry. Is that what you want to hear me say? Fine. I'm sorry. I made a mistake. People mess up, Zya. It happens. But you don't just throw them away. If you loved me, you'd have stayed to work it out."

"If I *loved* you?" Why was Zya just repeating everything he said?

Abby moved to stand in front of her and mouthed, *Are you okay?*

Zya nodded but wasn't at all sure she was okay. She needed to snap out of her shocked silence and give the man on the phone a piece of her mind.

"You did love me, didn't you, Zya?" Carter asked, his earnest tone full of hope.

"You have some nerve," Zya growled into the phone. "Did you really think you could just call me after all this time and demand that I come back to Salem? Did you expect me to just say, 'Okay, Carter. Of course, I will. I've just been waiting for you to show me you cared?'"

"Um, is it bad if I say yes?" he asked, obviously trying for humor.

It didn't work. She scowled into the phone. "Who do you think you are, Carter? I have a life here. A house. A business. Friends. You think—"

He cut her off. "And Brody Saxon."

There was dead silence between them as his words sank in. Finally she said, "So that's what this is about. You found out Brody is here and decided now it's time to try to get me back? That's really pathetic, Carter. You know that, right?"

"You want to talk about pathetic? How about you being engaged to me while simultaneously pining away for him. A man you'd never even dated. Why do you think I had to find comfort outside of our relationship, Zya? Because you were always waiting for him. Not me."

Zya pulled the phone away from her ear and stared at it, trying to determine whether this call was real or if she was dreaming it. She glanced at Yvette and Abby, both of whom were standing just a few feet away, clearly concerned about her. Then her rage hit her. She pressed the phone back to her ear and snapped, "You arrogant piece of pure trash. You're blaming me for your infidelity? Seriously? Not only are you blaming me, but you're demanding I come back to you. Well, let me be perfectly clear, Carter. I will never get back together with you, and this is my home now, so you're wasting your time. Goodbye."

Before she could pull her phone away from her ear, she heard Carter say, "You'll run from him, too. You always run."

It was his words that made her freeze. What he said was true. Zya *was* a runner. It's what she did when things got overwhelming. But this time was different, wasn't it? She'd opened her own business. She had her own home. And she'd made friends in Keating Hollow. Besides, it wasn't like she and Brody were actually dating. She wasn't going to run from her best friend.

"You don't know what you're talking about, Carter. Goodbye. Don't call me again."

"I'll tell them everything," Carter threatened. "Do not hang up on me, or the next call I'll make will be to Brody's parents."

She froze, her entire body going numb. "Exactly what are you going to tell them, Carter? That I left you after finding you in bed with their neighbor's daughter?"

He let out a humorless laugh. "That's old news. No one cares about that anymore. But we both know they'll care very much to hear about your arrest record. How do you think that's going to go over during that custody battle?"

"You sick bastard," she hissed out, regretting that night with every fiber of her being. Both the one where she'd ended up in police custody and the one when she'd told Carter. "I never would've guessed that even you would stoop so far. You do understand what happens to that little girl if Brody's parents get custody of her, don't you?"

"Sure I do. She'll grow up with every privilege. She'll want for nothing. I don't think there's a better place for her. And as a bonus, your little boy toy will suffer for all the garbage I've had to put up with over the years. I swear, Zya, you should've just flown to Paris and boned him however many times it took to get him out of your system, then you could've come home to me and finally given me all of you. That's all I ever wanted. That's all I want now. It's your choice. I'll be in touch."

The call went dead and Zya very carefully placed the phone onto the counter before tipping her head back and screaming.

It was a few seconds before anyone spoke.

"Zya?" Abby asked tentatively. "What can we do?"

Zya blinked a few times and then caught the scared expressions on her friends' faces and groaned. "I'm sorry. I'm just so angry. That bastard threatened me and is willing to sacrifice Winnie in order to get what he wants."

"He threatened Winnie?" Abby was already pulling her phone out, no doubt to call her deputy sheriff brother-in-law, Drew Baker.

"Not directly," Zya said quickly. "But his actions could hurt Brody's custody case. If I don't do what Carter wants, he'll supply information to Brody's parents about my past that could blow everything up."

Yvette raised both eyebrows. "Information about your past? What did you do, rob a liquor store?"

Zya winced. "Not on purpose."

"Oh, hellfire," Yvette said, pressing her fingertips into her eye sockets. "You have a record."

"It's supposed to be sealed," Zya said, starting to panic now. "I was visiting my grandparents in North Carolina and was a dumbass seventeen-year-old who was in the wrong place at the wrong time and clearly with the wrong guy. I was on probation until I turned eighteen. No one back home knew about this. I only told Brody, and then much later, I made the mistake of telling Carter. This shouldn't be an issue."

"It shouldn't," Abby agreed, frowning. "But if he tells Brody's parents, what are the chances they can get their hands on that police record?"

"Very high," Zya confirmed. "They are just like Carter. They'll stop at nothing to get what they want. Trust me. This is bad. Very bad."

"We're here for you, Zya," Abby said.

"That's right," Yvette said. "If your ex wants to come for you, he's going to have an entire town full of witches he has to go through first." She buffed her nails on her jeans. "Right, Abs?"

"Absolutely," Abby said, her voice firm.

Zya covered her face with her hands, trying to keep herself from screaming again. What in the hell was she going to do?

Abby scooted around the counter and pulled Zya's hands away from her face and said, "Look at me."

Zya did as she was told.

"You're not alone in this. Understand?"

"Yes." Zya stared at the two women and knew they weren't messing around. If she needed them, they'd come running with friends and family in tow. "But what do I do now? Just wait to see if Carter blows up our lives?"

"You need to tell Brody about it," Yvette said gently. "All of it. The call today and Carter's threats to use Winnie as a pawn to get what he wants. From there, you need to make a plan together. Like real partners."

Partners. When Zya had been engaged to Carter, neither

labels nor rings had meant anything to her. But now, if Brody gave her a ring, she knew she'd wear it for the rest of her days, completely committed to the only man she'd ever loved. "Partners," she whispered softly. "Yeah, I can do that."

"Good. Now go on. Before you lose your nerve," Yvette insisted and started to steer her out of the store.

Zya grabbed her purse, and after hastily locking up without selling even one thing to her friends, she jumped into her Jeep and hurried home to Brody and the sweetest little girl who'd already stolen her heart a thousand different ways.

CHAPTER 15

*B*rody pulled into the driveaway of Zya's house and frowned when he spotted Zya's Jeep parked in front of her garage. He glanced at the clock on the console, wondering if time had slipped away from him. It hadn't. Normally she would still be at the store when he and Winnie arrived after daycare.

"Looks like Zya is already here," he told his daughter, who was in the backseat.

"Zya's here?" she asked, her face lighting with interest.

"Yep. Wanna go see what she's up to?" He put the truck in park and jumped out before she could answer. When he opened the back door, Winnie was already reaching for him.

"Zya!" Winnie called, clearly excited to see her.

He chuckled. As soon as he got her out of her seat and onto her feet, she ran up the front steps and barreled into the house. When he'd been childless, he likely would've been annoyed at the loud outbursts and unchecked energy his daughter often displayed. But seeing her so happy, so full of life and wonder, just made him so utterly joyful, he didn't even recognize his former self.

With Winnie's backpack in hand, he walked into the house to find Winnie sitting on Zya's lap, the two of them already discussing Winnie's day at school.

He grinned at his friend, dropped Winnie's backpack off in her room, and then went into the kitchen to start working on dinner. He kept picturing Walter and Mary as they hurried out of his office that afternoon. Their obvious love for each other and easy rapport was enviable. Not to mention the fact that they were going on over three decades together and still acting like teenagers.

Could he have that with Zya? *Yes.* The answer was right there, pinging in his mind. He knew he could. But did she want that, and had they both changed enough that they wouldn't mess it up?

"Brody?" Zya said from behind him. He put the onion down that he'd been getting ready to chop and turned to find her standing there, wringing her hands.

"What's wrong? Is it Winnie?" He was already moving to go find his daughter.

"No, no." Zya shook her head. "Winnie's fine. She's on the couch, petting Lyra."

Brody glanced past Zya and spotted his daughter, happily talking to the cat about all the adventures they were going to have. He heard something about a magic carpet ride and smiled. But when he glanced back at Zya, her expression was so serious that he immediately sobered. "What's going on, Zy?"

She glanced at the table and closed her eyes as she asked, "Can we sit?"

"Sure." He grabbed her hand and led her over to the table.

"Let me get you something to drink. You look like you need a pick-me-up."

"You have no idea," she said and slid into one of the chairs.

"Coffee? Wine? Whiskey?" he asked.

She chuckled softly. "Maybe just water."

Okay, that wasn't like her. Not at all. But he hurried and got her some water and then grabbed the pink box on the counter that had an Incantation Café sticker on it that she must have brought home that afternoon.

Once he sat, he tapped the box. "Was this for something special?"

"Yes," she said, sounding wary.

He raised both eyebrows. "Did I forget someone's birthday?" He frowned in concentration. "It's not yours. That's for sure."

"No. Nothing like that." She let out a nervous laugh. "They're for you and Winnie. After this week, I thought you could use a treat."

He smiled gently at her. "That was really nice of you. Thanks, Zy." He sat across from her and handed her a cupcake. "It looks like you need one of these more than I do. Wanna tell me what's going on?"

She took the cupcake and peeled off the paper wrapper but didn't make an effort to eat it. Instead, she placed it on a napkin and gave him a pained expression.

"Zya," he said, trying to downplay his panic. "You're starting to worry me a little bit here. Are you okay?"

"No. I don't think I am," she said, her voice hitching.

Brody didn't think. He just acted on instinct. Zya wasn't a fragile person. In fact, she'd always been a pillar of strength. But this person sitting in front of him was anything but strong. In fact, she looked fragile, as if she might break at any moment.

He rose and hurried to her side, pulling up a chair so that he could sit right next to her. He didn't waste time wrapping an arm around her shoulders and pulling her in so that her head was resting against his chest. "Whatever it is, you can tell me."

"It's Carter," she whispered. "He called today."

Brody stiffened. "Carter?"

She nodded but didn't look up at him. "He wants me to go back to Salem."

"That's ridiculous. Is he out of his mind?" Brody wrapped his other arm around her, refusing to give any credence to the idea that she was considering her ex-fiancé's request. She couldn't go. Her business was in Keating Hollow. Plus she had her friends and now Brody and Winnie.

"Yes, he is," she said and lifted her head, meeting his gaze. "That's why I need you to tell me what you want me to do."

He blinked at her. "You want me to tell you what to do? Obviously, I want you to stay far away from that narcissist. Zya, what in the world would make you think I'd tell you to go back to him?"

She swallowed. "There's something I have to tell you."

"Okay," he said, with his heart beating too fast. Whatever she had to say, it was important. He'd never seen Zya like this before. She wasn't herself and it was really throwing him for a loop. "I'm listening."

She sat stiffly, staring at her hands as she said, "Do you remember when I was seventeen and went to visit my grandparents in North Carolina?"

"Yes," he said hesitantly. That had been a rough summer for Zya. And for him when he'd found out she couldn't come home until her probation ended in October. He'd been furious at the jackass who'd gotten her into legal trouble and almost ruined her future. It was only because her parents had hired a shark of a lawyer that she'd gotten out of that situation relatively unscathed. "Has that guy gotten in touch with you or something?"

"Huh? Oh, no." She shook her head. "It's actually worse than that. Or it could be."

Brody was silent as he waited for her to continue.

"Um, the only other person I told about that incident was Carter. Obviously that was years later, but if I was going to marry him, I figured he should know that was in my past."

"Yeah, I can see that. I guess." He didn't really. That had happened when she was a minor and it was over. In Brody's opinion, it wasn't anyone's business but hers.

"Carter is using that to blackmail me into going back to him," she blurted.

"Blackmail?" Genuine confusion washed over Brody. "How? Does he think people in Keating Hollow are going to boycott your business or something? I just don't think the people around here would punish you for something that happened when you were still a kid."

"He's not going to expose me to the people of Keating Hollow," she said. "He's going to tell your parents. You know what they'll do with that information. We can't risk it."

An ice-cold shiver crawled up Brody's spine while hatred filled his soul. A muscle started to tick in his neck, and Brody seriously wondered if his head was going to explode right there in her kitchen. "No."

"No what?" she asked, sounding a little more like herself now that she'd told him what was on her mind. "There's no way to stop him from telling them, Brode."

"I mean no, you're not going back to Salem to protect me. I won't allow him to blackmail us like that." There was no changing his mind. He would not let Zya sacrifice herself because her past might reflect badly on him.

"But Winnie—" she started.

"Zya, let me deal with my parents, okay? I really do appreciate everything you've tried to do for us. But I will not let this happen. You have a life here. I won't be responsible for ruining it. We'll just have to talk to Lorna and find out the best way to navigate this."

"I just want what's best for Winnie," Zya said, looking miserable. "She doesn't deserve to be in the middle of any of this."

Brody cupped one of her cheeks, staring her in the eyes. "Do you know what I want? More than anything?"

"For your parents to drop this lawsuit?"

It was a reasonable answer, but not what he'd been thinking. "Okay, yes, I do want that, but we both know that's not going to happen, so we'll just have to fight it. Besides that, what I want more than anything is for me and Winnie to have a life here in Keating Hollow… with you."

She nodded slowly. "I'll always be in your life, Brody. You know that."

He shook his head. "That's not what I mean, and I think you know it."

She glanced at his lips for just a second before meeting his gaze. "Brody?"

"Zya."

Her eyes flickered with an emotion he couldn't quite name. "I think you're going to have to explain exactly what you're saying here."

"You really need me to spell this out?" he asked, sort of amused now.

"Yes."

"Okay." He stood, pulling her to her feet with him. Moving in close, he wrapped his arms around her, and when his lips were only an inch from hers, he said, "I want you as more than a friend. That kiss we shared? I want to wake up to them and fall asleep to them. I don't want to put on a show for the town, and I sure as hell don't want anything between us to be a lie. I love you, Zya." He let out a soft chuckle when her eyes widened with shock. "Come on. You have to have known on some level that there's always been more between us. I'm not crazy, am I? Please tell me I'm not the only one who feels this spark between us."

Her chest rose and fell as her breathing sped up. Tears filled her green eyes. One tear fell, and Brody gently brushed it away with his thumb.

"Are these good tears or bad tears?" he whispered, feeling his chest tighten with his own out-of-control emotions.

She shook her head but then nodded as she let out a half laugh, half sob. Then she grabbed his face and covered his lips with her own. The kiss was gentle, a little tentative, just as it had been the day before. But as soon as Brody teased the seam of her lips, she opened for him and years of pent-up passion exploded.

Brody buried his hands in her long hair as he deepened the kiss, reveling in her sweet strawberry taste. There was no denying he wanted more. He wanted to touch her everywhere. To lift her up and carry her into his bedroom so that he finally, *finally* could explore every inch of the woman he'd wanted for as long as he could remember.

Zya seemed to be just as impatient as he was. She'd plastered herself to him, one hand sliding down his back while the other clutched at his short hair.

"Lyra!" His daughter's voice echoed through the house and

was quickly followed by the sound of small footsteps bounding through the living room.

Brody and Zya sprang apart, each of them breathing heavily. Zya's lips were slightly swollen, making Brody let out a tiny groan of frustration. She looked so sexy like that, and he suddenly had deep remorse that he'd been missing out on seeing her like that for far too many years.

The cat darted into the kitchen with Winnie following, her hands stretched out as if she was going to catch the cat.

Brody quickly scooped Winnie up into his arms. "Whoa there, little one. What did I tell you about running in the house?"

"No running," she said automatically.

"Right. And no chasing the cat, remember?"

His daughter pushed her bottom lip out, pouting as she nodded solemnly.

Brody couldn't help but laugh. "You're gonna be a lot of trouble in a few years, aren't you?"

"No!" she exclaimed, obviously offended by his comment.

"Oh, okay, sweetie pie. Good to hear it." He gave her a loud kiss on her cheek. "If I put you down, are you going to stop running?"

She nodded vigorously. Still, the moment her feet touched the floor, Winnie rushed to Zya and hugged her legs. "I love Lyra."

Zya caressed his daughter's hair as she smiled down at her. "Lyra loves you too, sweetheart. That's why she's been sleeping with you." Zya lifted her gaze and gave Brody a sheepish grin. "Sorry. I spotted the cat running into your room and went after her, only to find her snoozing away with you both."

Brody wanted to tell Zya he'd have been happy if she'd climbed in with them all, but he held his tongue. He needed to get his libido in check. His usual flirting tactics needed to be benched while his daughter was around. Instead he just said, "No apologies required, Zy. Winnie's already invading me every night, and now so is Lyra. At least you didn't wake me up."

"I try to be a good housemate," she said as she moved into the kitchen and started pulling ingredients out of the cabinet. "How about you return the favor and help me get dinner started. Otherwise, one of us is going to get pretty cranky, and I'm not talking about Winnie."

"I'm well aware," Brody said. "I was there the day of the epic meltdown at the pier, remember?" During college, they'd taken a trip to the beach, but they got stuck in traffic and had arrived much later than planned. Zya had been right at her hangry breaking point when the food shack had closed suddenly, leaving them high and dry. Zya had been so far gone that she'd made a full-grown man cry, chewed out two police officers, who'd opted to retreat rather than deal with her, and had nearly knocked down an elderly woman in a crosswalk as she tried to get to a pub a few blocks away.

"Did you have to bring that up, Brody?" Zya asked. "I'd just about wiped it from my memory and now here you are, burning it back into my brain."

"Sorry." He kissed her cheek, unable to keep away from her now that he'd poured his heart out to her. "We won't speak of it again."

Zya brought her hand up, covering her cheek where his lips had just been. Brody's heart swelled with love when he noticed the soft look on her face. It was an expression he'd spend the rest of his life looking for… if she'd let him.

CHAPTER 16

Zya stood at the sink, staring out at the darkness as she rinsed her mug. Her mind was buzzing with contradictions. On the one hand, her heart was so full, she thought it might burst right open. Brody had chosen her. He'd stood there in her kitchen and refused to let her sacrifice her life in Keating Hollow for him and Winnie. He'd finally voiced the words she'd always longed to hear. It had been like a dream. One she hoped she'd never wake from.

But none of that changed the fact that Carter had threatened her. Zya knew her ex was petty and jealous enough to tell the Saxons about her arrest. And like her grandfather had told her, trouble was coming.

"I think that mug might be clean now," Brody said, coming up behind her and turning the water off. His arms encircled her waist and he nuzzled her neck affectionately. "You're thinking too much, Zy."

"How can I not?" she asked as she put the mug in the dish drainer. Then she leaned back, letting her head rest on his shoulder. "My ex is going to make trouble for us. It'll be my fault if the custody hearing doesn't go your way."

"Your fault?" He tightened his grip on her, holding her close. "Baby, it will 100% be my parents' fault. Or mine if the judge decides I'm not doing a good enough job with my daughter. But never yours. All you did was give us a place to stay and love us."

Baby. The word sounded both strange and beautiful coming from his lips. But it also made her heart soar. She cleared her throat and forced a teasing tone. "Did I say anything about love?"

He quickly spun her around, keeping her trapped between him and the sink. His gaze was intense as he said, "Tell me, Zya. Do you love me?"

That electric current between them had her entire body buzzing. She wanted to touch him everywhere. Finally run her fingers over his bare skin, feel every dip and ridge of his muscular body, and learn it like it were her own.

"Don't ever stop looking at me like that, Zy," he said roughly.

"Like what?" she asked, running her hands up his chest, feeling his hard pecs through his T-shirt.

"Like you want to devour me."

She let out a tiny groan. "I never was one for a poker face."

He chuckled softly. "If that's the case, then why haven't I ever seen you quite like this before?"

Zya ran her finger lightly over his lips just because she could, and she shivered with desire when he sucked the digit into his mouth and bit down gently. Goddess above, what she wouldn't do to feel his mouth everywhere. "Um, is Winnie asleep?"

He released her finger and nodded. "She passed out before I finished reading the first book. You still haven't answered me."

She didn't have to ask what answer he was waiting for. She hadn't forgotten his question. How could she? Zya knew that once she voiced her truth, that'd be it. Her heart would be his forever. There was no going back. Not for her. She was either all in or she had to end this now. But ending it wasn't an option. There was no way she could walk away from him. From Winnie. Her breath caught as she looked up into his brilliant blue eyes. "I've always loved you, Brody. Always."

He gently tucked a lock of her hair behind her ear and held her gaze as he demanded, "Tell me you're in love with me, Zy. That you won't run when things get hard. Because we both know it's coming."

Her pulse was fluttering as she whispered, "I'm in love with you, Brody. I'm all in with you and Winnie." The tears were back as emotion overwhelmed her. But she blinked them back as she said, "I won't run if you won't."

His hands came up, roughly cupping her cheeks. His gruff voice was barely a whisper when he said, "Baby, the only time I'll be running is if it's to go after you."

The tears won the war, spilling over as Brody kissed her as if sealing their promises to each other. This time his kiss was slow and tender, full of love. Zya clung to him, happy to live in this moment forever. She felt loved and cherished as she let herself get lost in him.

When Brody finally pulled away, he grabbed her hand and led her into the living room where they snuggled up together on the couch. With his arm around her, she rested her head on his shoulder like she'd done hundreds of times before. Only this time, she was free to slip her hand into his, twine their fingers together, and know that he was finally hers.

"Brody?"

"Yeah?"

She glanced up at his handsome face. "Where do we go from here?"

He raised a questioning eyebrow and then gave her a sexy half smile. "The bedroom?"

Her body tingled with long pent-up anticipation. Damn. The man did things to her. "I didn't mean that." She shook her head. "I mean how are we going to navigate this with Winnie? She seems to be doing so well, and I don't want this or anything else to derail her progress adjusting to her new life."

His cocky expression turned to one of pure love. "That right there. That's why I love you. You're always putting those you care about first. Do you have any idea how special that is?"

"You're biased, I think," she said, placing a hand over his heart. "You just think that because you've always been my number one. So your perception might be a little skewed."

"Oh, yeah? What about when you first got together with Carter? Before you knew what a jackass he is?"

"Even then. Did you know that his excuse for cheating on me was because of our relationship? He told me that he always felt like a consolation prize."

Brody's expression darkened. "That guy has some nerve blaming you for his betrayal. He cheated because of his own insecurities, Zya. Not because of anything you did or didn't do."

"I know," she said softly. "But that doesn't change the fact that you've always been my favorite person. He knew it and was jealous. While I'm not letting him blame me for his infidelity, I am taking responsibility for the fact that the man I promised to marry didn't have my full heart. I gave away a part of it a long time ago and just never got it back."

"Zya," he breathed. "Why did we waste so much time?"

"I guess we just weren't ready for this," she said. "Whatever it is."

"Whatever this is? Are you saying you don't know?" He frowned at her, appearing confused. "Haven't I been clear about wanting you as my partner?"

Zya disentangled herself from him and scooted back into the corner of the couch, needing a little bit of space to get through this conversation. "Yes, I got that part. I'm just saying I think we need to talk about how to proceed. How do you want to handle this with Winnie? I mean, I don't think you can just sleep in my bed. She comes looking for you practically every night."

His lips curved into a pleased smile. "I see. So this is about sleeping arrangements. I understand now."

"Not just the sleeping arrangements." She tossed a throw pillow at his head. How could he be so endearing when he was insufferable? "Don't you think we should talk about how to present this to Winnie?"

"Present what?" he asked, waving a hand around the room. "She already knows and loves you. We share a house, and she hasn't had any trouble with that. The only thing that's changed here is the status of our relationship, and I honestly don't think she'll even notice. It's not like she knew me and her mother as a couple. So the problems that come with introducing a new partner just aren't there. So really, the only issue here is where I sleep. So now we're back to sleeping arrangements. Right?"

"You're evil. You know that, right?" She gave him an exasperated look but couldn't deny that he had a very good point.

"That's just one of the reasons you love me." He reached out and touched her face lightly. "Do you have any idea how much it amuses me when you look at me like that?"

Her lips twitched as she tried to fight a smile. "Just tell me what you want to do. I assume you'll stay in your bedroom and I'll stay in mine?"

Brody groaned. "That is *not* what I want to do. Not at all."

She didn't either. The thought of trying to go to sleep when he was just down the hall sounded like torture. "I just don't want her confused when she walks into my room with us wrapped around each other."

"Yeah, that's a good point." He reached out and took Zya's hand in his. "Tonight we'll stay in our own beds. But tomorrow, I'll speak with her and explain that you and I will be sharing a bedroom from now on. I think she'll be fine."

"So," she said, pursing her lips. "You just assume I'm going to be sharing your bed? What kind of girl do you think I am?"

Brody scooted forward, boxing her into her corner and said, "I think you're my girl. And I'm going to have a lot of trouble keeping my hands off you. Is that going to be a problem for you?"

"Uh, let me think about it." Her body started to tingle with anticipation. She tapped her index finger against her temple and glanced away, pretending to be deep in thought.

"Let me give you a preview." Brody placed one hand on her thigh and slowly moved it upward.

She sucked in a sharp breath and had to fight to keep from throwing herself at him. This was all she'd ever wanted in life. To have Brody at her side and to be able to touch him any time she wanted. Finally, she was on the verge of that reality.

Brody doubled down and slipped his free hand underneath her shirt and used his thumb to caress the skin just above her waistline.

"Brody," she said under her breath. "This isn't fair."

"It wasn't meant to be." He leaned in, nuzzling her neck before dropping open-mouthed kisses over her collarbone.

"Okay. You win," she said as she let her head drop back against the couch, giving him more access. If he wanted to play dirty, she was game. Let him see how hard it was to resist this electricity sparking between them. "No problems here. None at all."

Brody let out a soft chuckle. "That's good to hear." Then he kissed her softly one last time before climbing to his feet.

Zya stared up at him, blinking in confusion. Was he really leaving now? "Where are you going?"

He glanced over at the clock on the wall. "To bed. Seven comes early."

"You're going to bed now?" she asked, her eyes wide with disbelief. "Seriously? After all that seduction, you're just going to leave me now?"

"If I don't leave now, I fear I won't at all." He let his gaze sweep over her, making it clear he wanted her. "I think a rain check is in order."

Zya sat up and straightened her shirt, trying hard to hide her disappointment. While she'd been the one advocating for waiting, that didn't mean she wouldn't have enjoyed a great make out session. "When?"

"When what?" he asked, clearly messing with her.

"Brody," she warned, giving him her annoyed face. Why did he love riling her up so much?

He coughed, covering up his chuckle. "Can you get away from the store early tomorrow?"

"How early?"

"I can be here at two-thirty. Winnie has a playdate with

Yvette's daughter, Skye. We'll have the house to ourselves for a few hours."

Zya popped up off the couch, grabbed his face with both hands, and kissed him so thoroughly that by the time she stepped away, he was completely breathless.

Brody reached to pull her back into his embrace, but she shook her head and jumped back.

"Nope. You're going to bed, remember? Goodnight, Brody." She turned and started to walk down the hallway, pleased with herself. If he wanted to play games, she was all in.

"Wait! What about tomorrow?" he called after her.

"Oh. Right. Yes, I'm pretty sure I can be here by two-thirty." She winked and waved her fingers at him. "Night, Brode."

Zya left him standing there in the living room, watching her walk away. She knew he'd make the rounds of her house, making sure everything was locked up tight before he called it a night. And while she'd never had an issue living alone as a single woman, there was something comforting about knowing that he was there, watching over her.

After taking her time in the shower and luxuriating in her nightly face care regime, she finally wrapped herself in her robe and snuck out to the kitchen to get a glass of water. On her way back, she spotted Winnie and Lyra already curled up next to Brody, all of them passed out in a peaceful slumber.

Her heart melted and her insides turned to mush. Zya had always loved Brody, but this newer dad version of her best friend was something else entirely. She could see them living this life until they were old and gray. Her soul burned for it.

She just hoped Brody knew what he was doing. Because if her past was the reason why everything exploded, the reason he lost his daughter, she was certain he'd never forgive her.

They'd be done before they ever started.

Zya clutched at her chest, trying to stem the sharp pain that pierced her heart with just the thought of losing everything she'd ever wanted.

With a sigh, she slipped back into the shadows of the hallway and made her way back to her room. After placing the glass of water on her nightstand, she climbed into her lonely bed, wishing she was in Brody's room with the two people she already considered her family.

CHAPTER 17

"*S*ee you next week!" Zya called to Ms. Betty and a few of her friends from the retirement village as they started filing out the door. They came in every week after their spa appointments to check for new arrivals. Today they'd found a new crocheted shawl Zya had put out, and each of them had gone to town picking out colors to get started. It was going to be their weekly project.

Zya envied Ms. Betty and her friends. They were always so happy and full of life when they were shopping at her store. The joy they exuded was infectious, and she always had a good time when they were patronizing her shop. They were her favorite customers.

Ms. Betty paused at the door and glanced back at her. "Definitely. I have to finish burning through that cash in my pocket. That video of you and Brody was a hot commodity at the retirement village before it ended up all over the internet. If you ever want to make some extra cash, just let me know."

"Doing what? Filming make-out videos for your friends?" Zya asked with a laugh.

"Yes! You'd be surprised at how easily people throw down their cash when there are two hotties on the screen." She winked suggestively.

Zya's face flushed hot as she cleared her throat. "Uh, thanks for the suggestion, but I think Brody and I will probably pass on that offer."

"Too bad. Fresh content would've helped beef-up my yarn budget." She winked. "It's fine. I'll just go downtown and see if I can find any other lovebirds to film. Variety is the spice of life, right?" She held up two fingers in the peace sign and then flounced out of the shop, leaving Zya shaking her head.

With everything going on, Zya had actually forgotten about that video. It had just been a kiss. Nothing scandalous. She supposed she should be annoyed that Ms. Betty had charged her friends to view it, but at least the older woman had spent her proceeds at Witches in Stitches.

The door swung open and Zya glanced up to find Hope Garber walking into the store, chattering with a younger man and a preteen. Hope was wearing a faded *Nirvana* T-shirt and had her honey blond hair tied up in a messy bun. Her companions were dressed similarly in jeans and a T-shirt, only they were both wearing the same black shirt that had the band name *Silver Scars* written in script across the chest.

"Hope, hi," Zya said, smiling warmly at her. "I haven't seen you in a while." Hope was one of the Townsend sisters and was a massage therapist at A Touch of Magic Day Spa. "Been keeping busy?"

"You have no idea," she said with a laugh. "Between this one's extra-curricular activities"—she pointed at the young girl—"and working extra shifts to get ready for Levi's visit, I haven't had a moment to breathe in days. But now that Levi's here, I've got a couple of weeks off and I'm going to enjoy every minute of it."

"And that includes knitting?" Zya asked, amused as she watched the younger girl point out a skein of yarn to Levi. She held it up to her face and closed her eyes, enjoying the softness of the alpaca blend.

Hope chuckled. "Yes. These two said they wanted to learn to knit, so here we are."

Levi raised one eyebrow. "I did?"

"Fine. You didn't say you wanted to learn. But you didn't say you didn't want to either." Hope turned her attention back to Zya. "Frankie is the one who wants to learn, and she conned Levi into doing it with her."

Frankie stared up at Levi with adoration.

He shrugged and slipped his arm around her shoulders. "Come on, Frankie. Let's go find some yarn you like."

Hope watched them go with a tender look on her face. "He's so good with her."

"I didn't know you had a daughter," Zya said.

"Chad and I are fostering her. Frankie's been with us for about a month now." She leaned against the counter, still watching them, and then turned to Zya. "She's doing so great. If we get the opportunity, we will absolutely adopt her."

Zya had heard that Hope had spent some time as a ward of the state when she was a kid. It wasn't surprising that she'd be called to help other kids with her same background. "That's wonderful, Hope. She seems like a really nice kid."

"She is. Now, I'm gonna need a set of knitting needles and some beginner patterns to get her started."

"On it." Zya went to work gathering the items Hope needed while Levi and Frankie filled a basket with an eclectic mix of yarn. By the time they were done shopping, Zya had filled two large paper bags for them.

"I can't wait to see you wearing my scarf while you're out on tour, Levi," Frankie said.

"I'll wear it on my next album cover," he said as he made an X with his finger over his heart.

"You will?" Her eyes were wide. "But what if my scarf is ugly?"

"It won't be. But even if it is, so what? It's made by you. I'll love it anyway."

Goddess above. Were these kids real? She'd never been like that with her cousins when she was a kid. Not that Levi was a kid. He had to be in his early twenties. Maybe that was the difference. He was just so kind, and not quite what she'd have expected from a rising rock star. As she handed the bags to Hope, Zya turned her attention to Hope's brother. "Levi, are you playing anywhere while you're in town?"

He nodded. "Saturday at the farmers' market. It'll just be me, though. Seth is down in LA. So just an acoustic set."

"Wonderful," Zya said. "We'll make a point of swinging by."

Frankie placed her hand to the side of her mouth as if she were telling Zya a secret and whispered, "Silas Ansell will be there, too."

"Is that right?" Zya asked as she laughed at the pained expression on Levi's face.

"Frankie, I told you that was a secret," Levi admonished her.

"That's why I whispered it to her," the younger girl said, batting her eyes at him. "I was just trying to convince her to come see you play. It would be really embarrassing for my rock star brother if no one showed up," she teased.

Levi rolled his eyes and shook his head, but he wore an amused smile, and even though Zya was certain that Levi was mortified that his foster sister had spilled the beans about his actor boyfriend, Levi didn't seem to be upset. Instead, he seemed to be pleased that Frankie was having a good time. The pair seemed to have a special bond that was just really heartwarming to witness.

"Well, I'll be there. Wouldn't miss it," Zya said.

"Thanks." Levi shoved his hands into his front pockets. "Who's up for a trip to Incantation Café? I'm dying for a cappuccino."

"I am," Hope said. "Hanna's iced pumpkin bread is calling my name."

"Can I get a mocha frappe?" Frankie asked, rubbing her hands together. "Extra whip."

"Sure, kid." Hope slipped her arm through the girl's elbow as the three of them made their way out of the store.

"Nice to meet you!" Frankie called over her shoulder.

"You, too, Frankie," Zya replied. "See you Saturday."

The bell chimed as the door swung closed, and Zya glanced at the clock. It was just after two-thirty, making her already late for her date. She sent a quick text to Brody and then rushed around, closing up the shop for the day. Now that her shop was established, Zya was getting ready to hire someone to start in the spring, so she'd have help in the summer. Being that it was February, Keating Hollow wasn't yet inundated with tourists, and closing early wasn't much of an issue. It wasn't like people often had knitting or crocheting emergencies.

Zya wrote out a note for the front door, indicating that she'd be back at ten the next day, and then pulled out her keys. As she was locking up, an ominous chill crawled over her skin. She stiffened, already knowing what to expect when she turned around.

"Go away. You're not welcome here," she said and finished locking the door.

Brody is off limits, a raspy voice said from behind her.

"I said you're not welcome here," she said more forcefully as she spun, holding her hands up like a shield. The ghost was floating just a foot in front of her, wearing a trench coat and a fedora. His face would've been handsome if it wasn't for the scowl and the jagged scar that ran from the top of his eye down to his jawline.

It's not for you to say where I go, Zya Rossi, the ghost said.

Zya took a step back. "How do you know my name?"

I've been watching you.

"Why?" she asked as she concentrated on drawing her power to her. Her fingers twitched, trying desperately to connect with her magic, but it wasn't forthcoming. She didn't even feel the normal spark at her fingertips. What in the name of the goddess was happening? She normally was stronger when she was near water, but that didn't mean she needed it to create just a flicker of power.

You're messing with the wrong family.

She frowned, trying to ignore the ripple of fear washing over her. Without her magic to banish the spirit, she had no idea what would happen. Most ghosts were relatively harmless, but not all of them. And this one had all of her defenses up. "Are you still talking about Brody?"

Your family isn't good enough for the Saxons.

Okay. Now that was just rude. There was no doubt that Brody's parents had sent this spirit to frighten her. Why else would a random spirit just arrive out of nowhere to try to scare her? "The hell we aren't. This isn't the Victorian era, old man. People don't give a crap about status and social climbing around here. Tell Brody's parents to take their elitism and shove it where the sun doesn't shine."

You have this one chance to denounce your involvement with Brody Saxon, or I'll make that choice for *you.*

Zya sneered at the spirit. "Go away. You're not relevant here." She started to stalk off, determined to try to put some distance between them. To get closer to the river where she'd be able to draw on her magic, but as soon as she turned her back to the spirit, the ghost slammed into her. Her body went rigid as an ice-cold sensation paralyzed her. Her lungs didn't work, and her heart seemed to have just stopped.

I'm dying. This is what it feels like to die, she thought, panic taking over. But she couldn't control anything. Her magic was gone. Her limbs were heavy and unresponsive. She couldn't even breathe. She just stood there, horror crashing through her.

Brody's face materialized in her mind. His handsome smiling face, with brilliant blue eyes. But his expression quickly turned from the easygoing guy she'd loved her entire life to one that was angry. A vein had popped out on his forehead, and his eyes were bloodshot when he opened his mouth and snarled, *Welcome to hell.*

Zya was powerless as her body turned in the opposite direction and stalked down Main Street. There was a dull buzzing in her head and her movements were jerky. The spirit was controlling her, and there was absolutely nothing she could do. She wanted to break down and scream, shout, cry out for help. But she just couldn't. The only thing she had was her mind. She had to stay alert and be ready for any break in the spirit's possession of her body. If she could just reach for her magic. Concentrating with everything she had, she called to her power once more.

A sharp pain stabbed her fingertips, snuffing out the tiny spark of magic she'd managed to access.

Brody's bloodthirsty face appeared again in her mind. *You'll pay for that.*

He was gone just as fast as he appeared. Her mind was full of rage and fear and frustration at being animated by another being with no end in sight.

The spirit stopped her right in front of A Spoonful of Magic, the chocolate shop owned by a lovely woman named Miss Maple. After peering in, Zya's hand pulled the door open and she walked in, nearly stumbling over the threshold.

"Zya!" Miss Maple grinned from behind the counter. "I haven't seen you in a while. What can I get you?"

Zya couldn't open her mouth to speak, and the spirit didn't bother to answer Miss Maple. Instead, the next thing Zya knew, the spirit had reached into her bag and pulled out a pair of knitting needles. Clutching them in her hand, Zya boldly walked behind the counter and grabbed the older woman, fumbling to put her in a headlock.

"What the—" Miss Maple spun, tripped over Zya's feet and went down hard, taking a tray of chocolates with her.

The spirit forced Zya to scramble so that she was straddling the older woman. She stared down at Miss Maple, feeling the knitting needles in her hand and wanting to die right there. In no world would she ever attack anyone, especially not Miss Maple.

A war cry that wasn't initiated by Zya flew from her lips as her hand came down with such force that Zya was certain the knitting needles would be considered a deadly weapon. Only before they connected with Miss Maple's neck, Zya was hit with an invisible force that sent her flying up and over the counter and into the middle of the shop.

Zya landed flat on her back, the wind knocked out of her. But the ghost wasn't done. One second later, she was back on her feet, storming the counter again.

"Zya Rossi, I command you to stand down," Miss Maple said. "Drop the needles!"

The magic swirled around Zya and concentrated on her hand, slowly prying back one finger at a time from the weapons.

The door swung open and the next thing Zya knew, she was wrapped in strong arms. Immediately, the paralyzing effect dissipated and Zya started to breathe again, her lungs gasping for air as if she'd been drowning.

"Are you okay?" the familiar voice asked.

"No," she gasped out, immediately dropping the knitting needles and clutching at her throat. Zya's knees gave out, and if her savior hadn't been holding her, she'd have sunk right to the floor.

"Zya! Miss Maple!" Hope rushed past Zya and skirted behind the counter. She wrapped her arm around Miss Maple. "What happened?"

"Zya attacked me," Miss Maple said, her voice shaking.

"It's not her fault." The man who was holding Zya released her and moved to stand beside her.

She glanced over and spotted Levi Kelley.

He put his hand out, indicating that she should take it. "It'll help keep the spirit away."

Zya immediately grabbed his hand and felt a little stronger for it.

The door burst open and before anyone could say anything else, Drew Baker was there, his gun drawn and aimed right at Zya.

Zya immediately put her hands in the air.

"What happened?" he demanded.

"Zya came in and suddenly attacked me with her knitting needles," Miss Maple said.

Drew's gaze landed on the discarded needles and then on Zya's face. "Did you attack Miss Maple?"

Zya nodded, a sob clogging her throat. "It was me, but—"

The deputy didn't let her finish and wasted no time pulling out his handcuffs and reading Zya her rights. Her body went cold again, and she started to fear that the spirit would materialize again.

"She was possessed," Levi said. "It's not Zya's fault."

Drew glanced between the two of them and then said, "I still have to take her in, Levi. We'll have to sort it out there."

Levi nodded and reached for Zya's arm again. His touch soothed her, made her feel stronger as if he was forming a barrier to keep her safe from the spirit.

"Deputy Baker," Miss Maple said. "Thank you for coming so quickly."

"Of course. We're lucky I was in the office when the silent alarm went off." He clutched Zya's arm. "Let's go. I'll get everyone's statement once we get back to the office."

As she moved forward, Levi was forced to let go, and Zya couldn't help but look back at him. Just before she was led out the door, she mouthed, *Thank you.*

Levi nodded, his expression troubled.

CHAPTER 18

*B*rody stepped out of the shower, humming to himself. The day had gone by surprisingly fast even though all he'd wanted to do was stay home and learn every inch of Zya's body. He'd gotten home about fifteen minutes after two and jumped right in the shower. After tending to the soil all morning out at the Pelsh winery, he hadn't wanted to smell like he'd been rolling around in the dirt when she got home.

Because he had plans. So many plans. And all of them included being as close as two people could be. He wrapped a towel around his waist, brushed his teeth, and then shaved. Just as he was pulling on his jeans, he heard his phone ping.

It was from Zya, indicating that she was on her way.

Anticipation tingled up his spine. He'd waited a long time for this moment with Zya. He was determined to make the most of it.

Brody headed into the kitchen and grabbed one of the red roses from the bouquet he'd purchased on the way home. They were Zya's favorites, and while he didn't want to go overboard with rose petals and candles everywhere, he did want to show her she was special.

As he was headed toward the hall that led to her bedroom, there was a sharp knock on the door. He frowned. Zya wouldn't be knocking. He quickly crossed the room and while still holding the rose, he pulled the door open and then blinked in shock. "Mother?"

"Brody," Blair Saxon said, holding a small overnight bag. She scanned him up and down. "Is this how you answer your door now? Half-naked?"

He ignored her question and in a cold voice asked, "What are you doing here?"

"I came to see Winnie and to resolve this custody suit. Are you going to invite me in?"

Brody wanted to slam the door in her face. He briefly considered it. But if there was a chance he could talk her into dropping the lawsuit, he had to take it. Silently, he stepped back and waved for her to enter.

She tentatively crossed the threshold, her eyes darting around the space.

Brody looked at the cozy living room through his mother's eyes and knew she'd disapprove. The home was a standard three-bedroom, two-bath house with a living room, dining room, and kitchen. It was a far cry from his parents' 4000 sq. ft. Victorian that was decorated with so many antiques he'd been convinced the place was haunted by at least a dozen ghosts.

Zya had made her living room comfortable with an overstuffed sectional, a matching chair, a red and gray area rug, and modern lamp fixtures. It was his mother's worst decorating nightmare. Brody, however, felt more comfortable in Zya's space than he ever had in his parents' home.

"This is where you're living now?" she asked, not even bothering to hide her disdain.

"There's nothing wrong with Zya's house," he said with a scowl. "Did you come here to insult us or to talk?"

"I didn't insult you." She gently set her bag onto the coffee table and then slowly lowered herself to the couch, sitting on the very edge as if it were dirty or contaminated.

Brody rolled his eyes. "I know you better than that."

"Brody," she said with a tired sigh. "Go put a shirt on so we can talk."

He considered refusing, but honestly, he felt like he could use the armor. Feeling vulnerable in front of his mother wasn't an option. He stalked out of the room and grabbed the first hoodie he found in his bedroom. When he returned, he stood in front of the couch with his arms crossed over his chest. "Okay. You wanted to talk. So talk."

"You don't need to be hostile, Brody."

He let out a derisive snort. "That's rich. You're the one who filed a lawsuit for custody of *my* daughter. And you're telling me *I* don't need to be hostile. Tell me, Mother, exactly how am I supposed to be behaving? Grateful that you're trying to destroy our lives?"

His mother stared him down with her brilliant blue eyes, the mirror image of his own, and with ice in her tone, she said, "Sit down, Brody."

He wanted to tell her that he wouldn't budge now even if fire were licking at his feet. But his rational side took over, and he forced himself to sit in the oversized chair across from the couch. Starting their meeting off by intentionally antagonizing her would kill any hope of talking her out of her ill-conceived lawsuit. "Did Dad make the trip with you?"

She shook her head and tucked a lock of her perfectly

styled dark hair behind one ear. "He had a business meeting he couldn't postpone, but we're both in agreement that we want to end this custody case."

"That's promising," he said, careful to keep his voice neutral. He didn't for one moment believe that his parents were dropping the custody battle without major concessions from him. Otherwise, she wouldn't be here.

"We really don't want to put you or Winnie through a court battle. You must know that, Brody."

He didn't answer. He was afraid if he did, he'd tell her exactly what he thought of them. Instead, he waited her out.

"I know you think we're awful." Her eyes turned bright with unshed tears, and she reached into her designer handbag to grab a monogrammed handkerchief. After dabbing at her eyes, she turned her face to him, showing off her red eyes and trembling lips.

This was all part of her manipulation. He'd seen it a thousand times before. When she wanted something that wasn't easy to get, she'd do her passive-aggressive routine to make him feel bad and ultimately cave to whatever she wanted. Not this time. She'd gone too far. Way too far. "How would you have felt if your parents had tried to take me from you, Mother? Wouldn't you think they were awful?"

She let out a half sob, half gasp. When she got her breathing under control, she stared him right in the eyes and said, "I never kept you from them. Your grandparents had the opportunity to see you whenever and wherever they wanted. There was no need to take you. They already had all the access they wanted."

They had? That was news to Brody. He barely remembered his grandparents and could count on one hand the amount of memories he'd made with them as a kid. "Okay.

I never said you couldn't see Winnie, though. So why are you doing this?"

"You moved her three thousand miles away, Brody! When was I supposed to see my granddaughter?" She had her hand over her heart, playing up her outrage.

"When you got on a plane to come see her. Why is that so hard? Millions of grandparents do it all the time. Just like you are right now."

Blair Saxon glanced around the room and then peered down the hall. When she finally turned her attention back to Brody, she asked in a hushed tone, "Where is she?"

"She who?" he asked, exasperated and ready to just hear what she wanted to say to him.

"Winnie. Shouldn't she be home from school by now? You didn't forget to pick her up, did you?" She was already getting to her feet when Brody held up his hand, indicating she should stop.

"I didn't forget to pick up Winnie. Damn, Mom." He shook his head, honestly wondering why he was ever surprised by what she said. "Winnie is at a playdate today. I'll get her around dinnertime."

"With who? You haven't even been here that long. How do you know you can trust these people? Winnie isn't safe with just anyone, Brody! You have to be careful. People—"

"Mom!" he barked.

She clamped her mouth shut and shook her head.

"That's better. Winnie's fine. She's with a schoolmate." Brody glanced at the clock, wondering what had happened to Zya. She'd texted that she was on her way at least fifteen minutes ago. It didn't take that long to get from her shop to her house. His fingers itched to text her, to make sure nothing terrible had happened to her. But he decided maybe she'd gotten back just in time to see his mother walk in the door. That would keep Zya away for sure. Hell, Brody couldn't even say what he'd have done if he'd had the choice to flee.

"Okay then," she said with a sniff. "I'm just concerned."

"You don't need to be." His hands had curled into fists and his knuckles were turning white. The tension in the room was enough to stifle him. He cleared his throat and consciously forced his hands into open positions. "Why don't you just tell me what you and Dad want."

"We just want to see our granddaughter," she insisted.

"Yeah, I got that part. But what is it you want me to change? My job is here. Winnie likes it here. And Zya is here. It's not like Winnie and I don't have a support system. The change has been good for us. Or it was until I got those court papers. So just let it out, Mom. What do you and dad want to make this custody battle go away?"

"We want you to come home, Brody. Why do you need to live all the way out here in this tiny little town when you could be back in Salem, working for your dad? The nannies could care for Winnie, and both of your lives will be easier. Family first."

"Family first?" he scoffed. "Suing for custody is putting family first? Your priorities are way out of whack, Mother."

"We only did what we felt we had to do." She stood, her eyes narrowed. "Are you saying you won't even consider moving back home? Not even to keep your daughter from being in the middle of a custody battle?"

Brody was so angry that he was shaking. But blowing up at his mother would only hurt his case. He clasped his hands together and stared up at her. "I will not let you weaponize my daughter. Understand?"

"That is not what we're doing," she said with an exaggerated sigh. "Stop being dramatic."

A growl rose up from the back of Brody's throat, but he forced himself to swallow it. "I'm the one being dramatic?" He let out a humorous laugh. "Please. You're the one who waltzed in here and told me you'd stop making my life a living hell if I'd only cave to your unreasonable demands. I think you should leave, Mother. It's time to just let our lawyers handle this one."

"You don't really want me to leave, Brody. Trust me." She crossed her arms over her chest and stared him down like she used to when he was a precocious kid.

"I do. It's time to go." He walked over to the door and held it open.

His mother grabbed her bag and walked over to him. But before she stepped outside, she grabbed his arm, clutching tightly, and said, "Family is everything Brody. And if you don't come home to us, your friend Zya is going to find out exactly what happens when someone comes between me and my own."

"What the hell does that mean?" Brody demanded.

"You'll find out soon enough, son. Now step aside. I've been asked to leave." She held her head up high and practically glided out of the house and down the stairs.

Brody clutched the door, determined to watch her leave. To make sure she wasn't going to just sit in her car until she saw any sign of Winnie.

The car's lights came on, and his mother hastily made a three-point turn. Once she was turned around, she sped down the driveway and disappeared. But not before the giant white wolf stepped out of the shadows, clearly watching to make sure she left. Once the car's taillights were no longer visible, the white wolf trotted over to Brody and sat right in front of him.

"Hey, boy," Brody whispered, more worried than ever. "Where is she?"

The wolf didn't even twitch an ear in acknowledgment.

Another ripple of fear slid down Brody's spine. The wolf never engaged with him. The wolf only cared about Zya.

"Where is she, boy?" he asked the wolf. "Do I need to get into the truck and go find her?"

The wolf let out a howl and then ran over to Brody's truck. He laughed but then quickly sobered. There wasn't anything funny about Zya being MIA. "Fair enough. If you want to help, get in. We're going to find her."

The wolf waited patiently for Brody to get the door open. As soon as Brody waved the wolf into the cab, he leaped up easily and sat on the passenger's seat, clearly ready to go find her.

Brody ran back into the house and grabbed his phone, his wallet, and another jacket. When he was on his way out, a call came in. He almost didn't answer it because it was an unknown caller, and he didn't have time for spam calls. But this one was local, and he knew it could be just about anything. Hastily, he hit accept and waited.

"Brody Saxon?"

"This is Brody."

"Brody, this is Levi Kelley, and I—"

"Levi Kelley, the lead singer of Silver Scars?"

"Yes," the man on the other end of the line said. "Only Seth is also a lead singer. It depends on the song."

"Sure," Brody nodded, even though the other man couldn't see him. "I don't mean to be rude, Mr. Kelley, but—"

"You're Zya Rossi's emergency contact, right?" Levi asked.

"Yes. Why? What's happened?" Brody's panic mode was fully engaged now. What had happened to Zya?

"I'm afraid I have some bad news."

Brody's body stiffened. "I'm listening."

"Zya has been arrested. You should get down to the sheriff's department as soon as you can."

"Arrested?" he bellowed. "For what?"

"Attempted murder," Levi said, whispering the news to him.

"Impossible!" Brody wanted to throw the phone or kick in a door. But he refrained and listened to Levi. "Who are they saying she tried to kill?" He rubbed at his chest, trying to make the ache go away.

"Miss Maple," Levi said. "Her only weapon was a pair of knitting needles, so I'm not sure she would've been successful trying to take down another witch."

"Miss Maple?" Brody was back to quoting the man after everything he'd said, just so that he could wrap his brain around it. "Why?"

"Because she was possessed by one of your ancestors. If you want to help Zya beat these charges, you'll come right now. We'll be waiting."

Brody didn't understand why Levi was the one calling him, but at that moment, he didn't care. All he knew was that he had to get to Zya's side immediately. "I'll be right there."

There was no hesitation. Brody hurried outside to find the wolf still waiting in the passenger seat of the truck.

"Let's go get her back, boy," Brody said to the wolf and then took off down the street, the back end of his truck fishtailing as he went around a curve.

CHAPTER 19

*Z*ya paced her cell, her insides numb. She still hadn't quite wrapped her head around what had happened. One minute she was headed home to Brody, and the next she was possessed by a ghost and attacking Miss Maple with knitting needles.

Her stomach rolled and she thought she was going to vomit. No one had told her anything since the deputy sheriff had brought her in. She'd been processed, allowed one phone call, and had been placed in her cell. Now she was waiting for Lorna White, the same lawyer who was helping Brody with his custody case, to show up so she could advise her on what would happen next.

There was no way she'd be let out. Zya knew that. She'd attacked someone. Or at least the spirit that had been possessing her had, but proving that would be a challenge, even with Levi as a witness.

She sat down heavily on the metal bench and buried her face in her hands. There were no tears. Just a deep despair that she thought might eat her alive.

"Zya?"

She jerked her head up and found Lorna White standing outside her cell with Deputy Sheriff Drew Baker beside her.

Zya rose and walked over to the door. "It wasn't me."

Lorna pressed her lips together in a thin line. "Don't say anything else right now."

She nodded.

Drew opened her cell and said, "You'll have a few minutes to talk to your lawyer before we interview you."

The three of them walked to a small room that had a wall of glass windows. Once Zya and Lorna were seated, the deputy sheriff left and closed the door behind him.

"Did you call Brody?" Zya asked, her stomach churning. She knew he'd be worried sick, and previously in their relationship, she'd expect him to support her in any way he could. But now that he had Winnie and the custody battle to consider, he couldn't afford to be anywhere near this. She'd asked Lorna to tell him to not get involved. To worry about his own case and not let hers interfere.

"I tried, but he didn't answer and then was already here when I arrived." She took out a legal pad. "Let's talk about what happened."

"Did you tell Brody to go home? I don't want him to get involved in this."

Lorna frowned at Zya. "Do you have any idea how serious this is? The sheriff is talking about attempted murder charges. Brody is the least of your worries right now."

"Right." It was just easier to focus on Brody than her current dire situation.

"Why don't you just start at the beginning and tell me what happened?"

"Yeah. Um, I was closing up my shop, and the next thing I

knew there was this spirit and—" Zya's eyes widened with horror as the spirit materialized right beside Lorna.

"What is it, Zya?" Lorna asked, glancing around.

"He's here," she whispered. "Right beside you."

Stop talking, Zya, the ghost ordered.

"No!" she cried and stood. "You aren't welcome here." Now that Zya knew what the spirit was capable of, she would not sit around and have a conversation with him while he tried to possess her again.

The spirit flew across the table, slamming into Zya, clearly trying to take possession again, only he couldn't. There was some sort of barrier that prevented him. Zya vaguely wondered if the sheriff's station had some sort of wards that prevented such a thing, but she had no time to voice the thought.

The spirit came at her again, this time wrapping his hands around her neck and lifting her up until she was pressed against the wall, her feet dangling above the floor.

Lorna let out a scream and started calling for the sheriff.

Zya clawed at the spirit's hands, trying and failing to release his grip. Her lungs burned and her eyes watered. Blackness started to creep in around the edges of her vision. Was this really how it was going to end? Was she going to die by the hands of a Saxon ancestor? She wanted to scream out for Brody. To make sure he knew she loved him, but she couldn't do anything at all as her life slowly slipped away.

"Zya!"

Strong arms wrapped around her as air rushed back into her lungs. Her feet hit the ground and her knees buckled, but someone was holding her up, keeping her from collapsing to the tiled floor.

"You're okay," Levi soothed, his lyrical voice calming her as the world started to come back into focus.

Zya opened her mouth to speak, but no words came out. She tried to clear her throat but ended up sucking in another deep breath.

"Ms. Rossi, do you need medical attention?"

Zya's eyes finally focused on Deputy Sheriff Drew Baker. He was standing behind Levi, his face white. The sheriff was shaken. She nodded once and pressed her hand to her throat.

Drew immediately tapped something on his phone and stepped just outside the of the room.

She met Levi's eye and croaked out, "What… happened?"

"The same spirit that was possessing you at A Taste of Magic was back and he attacked you," Levi said.

"I… know. How… you… what are you… doing in here?" Her speech was stilted, but at least she was communicating.

"Drew came and got me when he couldn't do anything about the spirit." Levi pulled out a chair for her. "Sit down. I'll get you some water."

Zya did as she was told and then looked around, finding her lawyer standing just outside the room, having a heated conversation with the sheriff. Lorna looked like she wanted to throw hands while the sheriff was just standing there with his arms crossed over his chest, saying very little.

A few moments later, Levi walked back in with a bottle of water. He handed it to her and took a seat next to her. "How are you doing?"

She shook her head. How was she supposed to answer that question? She couldn't. Not yet. Instead, she took a small sip of water and winced.

"If it helps, I'm pretty sure you're going to be released without any charges," he said.

"What? How?" she asked, a tiny bit of hope sparking in her heart. Ever since she'd been brought in, she'd been resigned that her life had imploded. That everything she'd worked for was gone and her life with Brody and Winnie had vanished into thin air. But if Levi was right... It was almost too much to hope for.

"Two things. Your lawyer is out there arguing that you can't be held responsible for what a spirit does, and since you have me, a witness to testify it wasn't you that attacked Miss Maple, then they can't charge you with anything. The second thing is that Miss Maple is out in the lobby throwing a fit about you being locked up. She refuses to press charges for assault. And if they charge you anyway, she's going to be a hostile witness. Which all means that any case they try to build against you is going to be seriously flawed."

"Miss Maple is out there?" Zya desperately wanted to go check on the older woman. Even though the spirit had taken over Zya's body, she still felt responsible.

"Yep. Once I explained to her what happened, she's been trying to get the sheriff to release you. Brody is also out there. He refuses to leave until you're released." Levi patted her leg. "Don't worry. You've got a small army of people behind you."

Brody.

He was there. Waiting for her. Tears pricked her eyes, but they cleared instantly when she spotted the spirit lurking on the other side of the glass where Lorna and the sheriff were still talking. "Levi, the spirit is back," she whispered.

"What?" He glanced around the room, but then stilled as his gaze followed hers. "He's out there because I'm in here."

"Huh? Why does that matter?" she asked, feeling as if she should know the answer, but couldn't quiet recall it.

"It's me and my magic," he said. "I've always been able to

181

sense other people even when I couldn't see them. It's true for spirits, too. They don't tend to like to hang around me because my energy usually sends them back to where ever they came from."

"You're a spirit witch?" she asked. Not all spirit witches had the ability to cast out ghosts, but some could. Though Levi's magic appeared to be stronger than most if he could exorcise a spirit out of her body just by touching her.

"I am. I'm also a healer as well as a singer." He gave her a shy smile. "Though I haven't been doing much healing since my music career took off."

"You are right now," she said, glancing down at his hand that was resting on her leg. A tiny shimmer of magic was being transferred from him to her. "I think that's why I'm speaking better."

He glanced down at his hand and then back up at her. "I didn't even realize I was doing that." Levi let out a low chuckle and shook his head. "That's not usually how I heal people."

"I didn't think so, but I appreciate it."

The door swung open and Lorna walked in with another woman Zya recognized as Gerry Whipple, one of the town heelers. Gerry was tall with short silver hair and kind eyes. She walked straight to Zya and sat down next to her. "Hi, Zya. I'm here to check you over for the sheriff. Is that okay with you?"

"Yes," she said, her voice still gruff from the near strangling.

The healer inspected her throat and then pulled back. "Are there any other injuries besides your throat?"

"I'm not sure," she said.

"She has a bruise on her shoulder and one on her hip," Levi said quietly.

Zya glanced down at her jeans and sweatshirt. "How do you know that?"

He grimaced. "I didn't until Healer Whipple asked, but it suddenly popped into my mind. I think it's that magical connection." He held his hands up, showing the faint trace of magic still sparking over them.

"Okay. Let me see what I can do," Gerry said. The healer placed her hands on Zya's throat and muttered an incantation. Zya's skin tingled with the soothing magic as it spread across her body. There was a minor sting as the magic healed her throat and then a few more once it reached her bruises. She winced, but then suddenly all her aches and pains were gone. "Sorry about that," Gerry said. "I should've warned you that would hurt a bit."

Zya rubbed at her throat one more time and was surprised it wasn't even a little tender. "It's okay. And thank you. Your magic is really impressive."

"I'm not sure I'd say impressive. Levi made my job easier." She patted Zya's hand. "I think you're going to be okay now. If you have any other issues pop up, don't hesitate to call me."

"If I'm allowed to, I will," Zya said, knowing full well that her situation was still dire.

"Well, if it comes to that, tell the deputy sheriff. He's a reasonable man." She held her hand out to Levi and then left the room.

The sheriff walked in. "Thank you, Levi. Your help has been invaluable."

"Sure," Levi said awkwardly as he glanced between them.

"You can go," the sheriff said.

Levi shook his head. "Sorry, Drew. No can do. The spirit is still here and if I leave, I'm pretty sure he'll attack Zya again."

The sheriff stiffened and then glanced around. "He is? Where?"

Levi pointed toward the door. "Out there. He's just standing there, waiting and watching."

The sheriff muttered a curse and then hung his head in frustration. Finally he let out a breath and said, fine. Stay for the interview, but only if Ms. Rossi consents.

Zya nodded quickly. "I do."

"Okay then." He turned to Levi. "Please just stay silent while I take Ms. Rossi's statement. If you have something to say, you can tell me after. Understand?"

"Sure."

The door swung open and Lorna walked back in. She took a seat next to Zya and said, "Zya, feel free to answer any of the sheriff's questions. If there is something I find questionable, I'll advise you to stay silent. Okay?"

"Yeah, okay." Zya didn't have anything to hide, but she also didn't want to complicate her case if she could help it.

As it turned out, Drew only had a few questions for her. The only ones Lorna wouldn't allow her to answer had to do with why Zya thought the spirit was targeting her. The lawyer argued that Zya couldn't possibly know why, and it wasn't her job to assign motive.

The deputy sheriff dropped that line of questioning and then stood. "Okay. You're free to go, but be advised that this case isn't closed. We will still be investigating this matter."

"I'm not being charged with a crime?" Zya asked, wanting to be sure she understood.

"Not today," the deputy sheriff said. "We'll be in touch if we need anything else from you."

Lorna handed him her card. "Call me if you need anything from my client."

He nodded and swept out the door.

"Let's go," Lorna said.

Zya glanced at Levi. "What do I do if the spirit follows me?"

"You're sticking with me for now," Levi said.

"That's kind of you, Levi. Thank you. I'm certain we can come up with a way to banish this ghost for good, then I'll be out of your hair," Zya said, grateful he was being so kind.

"Don't worry about it," he said. "I'm in this now. Might as well see it through." He winked and then led her out of the small room.

CHAPTER 20

*B*rody heard the footsteps coming down the hall and stopped his pacing. He saw Lorna first, then a tall younger man, and finally Zya.

Relief flooded through him as he strode across the room in three strides and pulled her into a tight hug. "Are you okay?"

"I am now," she said, burying her head into his chest. They stood there for what seemed like hours but had to only be seconds before she pulled back and looked up at him. "You shouldn't be here."

He scowled. "Of course I should be here. I'm your person."

Her expression softened, but then a shadow of raw pain flashed in her eyes. "You're also Winnie's person. You know this will get back to your mother. She'll use it against us."

"My mother can rot for all I care," he growled. When Brody had gone to bed the night before, he'd been wide awake with anticipation for this afternoon. He'd waited way too many years to finally make Zya his own. Today was supposed to be the day that they finally moved their relationship squarely into the couple zone. Instead, he'd had to deal with his mother's manipulative garbage and then had nearly lost his mind when he'd heard about Zya's ordeal. The only things he knew for sure were that he was not leaving Zya to deal with this by herself and that he'd fight his parents tooth and nail for custody of his daughter. "I'm not leaving you to deal with this by yourself. We're a team."

"But—" she started.

He put his hand up, pressing two fingers to her mouth. "No buts, Zy. If we were married, do you think I'd abandon you?"

"No." She shook her head. "This is different though. We're not married and we have choices. I don't want this to be harder for you."

He knew what she was saying. He even loved her for it. That didn't change anything for him, though. There was just a gut feeling that whatever had happened earlier, it was all too much of a coincidence. Zya had been dealing with ghosts and spirits her entire life. Why had one possessed her now, right when Brody was getting close to her? He couldn't shake the feeling that it was somehow because of him. "I've made up my mind, Zya. I'm not going anywhere. You're not being charged."

"Not yet at least," she said, staring down at her feet.

"Not ever if I have anything to say about it," Miss Maple declared as she came forward and pulled Zya out of Brody's arms. "How are you doing, honey? Are you hurt?"

Zya nodded, clutching the older woman's hands. "I'm okay. How are *you*? Did I hurt you?"

"Nothing a little trip to the healer won't fix," she said, rubbing her hip. "I'm a tough old broad." She winked at Zya. "The moment Levi told me what happened, I knew it must be true. You didn't look anything like yourself when you came after me. I would've almost sworn you were possessed, and

188

when Levi confirmed it, I knew I had to come down here and get the deputy sheriff to back off."

"He's backed off," Zya said with a grateful smile. "Thank you. You have no idea how much I appreciate you coming down here and advocating for me."

"I'm only doing what's right. When you're feeling up to it, come by the store. I'll hook you up with some amore chocolates. They're good for date nights if you know what I mean."

Zya hugged the older woman.

Miss Maple hugged her back and then moved on to Brody. "Take care of this one. Being possessed even for a short time is very rough on the psyche."

"I will," he promised. "Thank you. We appreciate you more than you know."

Miss Maple waved a hand, as if to say none of it was a big deal, and then left the sheriff's office.

Brody turned to Zya. "Are you ready to go home?"

"Uh, about that," she said, looking at Levi. "I have a ghost problem, and Levi seems to be the solution. I don't want to put Winnie in danger while I'm dealing with this, so going home isn't an option just yet."

Brody tried to wrap his head around what she'd just said but was still confused. "I think I'm missing some context."

Lorna White stepped in. "Let's get out of here and go to my office where we can talk." She glanced at Levi. "All of us."

"Okay." Brody grabbed Zya's hands in his, just needing the connection. "Levi, are you good to ride with us?"

"Sure. I came in with my sister, but she went home to deal with family stuff. I'll need a ride home anyway."

Brody nodded and then they all filed out of the police station and headed to the lawyer's office.

Ten minutes later, Zya and Brody were sitting at a conference table, while Levi stood by the window. Lorna brought everyone coffee and set out a plate of cookies.

"Levi, please have a seat," Zya said softly.

"I shouldn't be here for this conversation," he said. "But I also don't want to leave you alone in case the spirit shows up again."

"It's fine with me if you're here," she said and then turned to Brody. "We can leave while you talk to Lorna about the custody case."

"No." He squeezed her hand. "I don't have anything to hide. Levi can stay."

"All right. Let's get started." Lorna scribbled across her legal pad. "Zya, you told me back at the police station that the spirit that possessed you warned you about your relationship with Brody. Is that right?"

Brody stiffened. "What? Why?"

Zya turned to him. "He told me I wasn't good enough for the Saxon family and that I had one chance to denounce you. When I refused, he attacked me."

"Not good enough for the Saxon family?" Brody repeated, his blood running cold. "Are you saying the spirit is part of my bloodline?"

"It thinks so. Or he was called by someone in the Saxon family."

Holy mother-effing hell, Brody thought as his head started to pound. He pressed his fingertips to his temple and wanted to scream. "This can't be happening."

"Oh, it's very real, Mr. Saxon," Lorna said gently. "If what Zya says is true, then someone is doing everything they can to keep you two apart."

His head snapped up. "It's my mother."

Zya blinked at him. "Your mom? I'm sure she wouldn't send a ghost after me."

"Yes she would." He turned to her, cupping her face with one hand. "My mother is here in Keating Hollow, and she came to see me today while I was waiting for you to get home. She told me that if I moved back home with Winnie that she'd drop the custody agreement. When I refused, she threatened you. She said that if I didn't do what she wants, then you were going to find out the consequences. I'm convinced this is my mother's doing."

Lorna was scribbling furiously across her legal pad while Zya stared at him, her face white.

"I'm so sorry, baby," Brody said. "I'll handle this."

"No, you won't," Lorna said suddenly. "Do not under any circumstances speak to your mother again." She put her pen down. "Not until this is resolved."

"I can't just sit back and do nothing," Brody said. "She's trying to blackmail me and she's causing real harm to Zya."

"I understand," Lorna said with a sympathetic smile. "But blowing up at her won't help your case. Instead, we need to find proof that she is sabotaging your life. Does your mother have magic that can compel spirits?"

"Not that I know of," he said. "But that kind of thing isn't that hard to come by in Salem. And since Zya is from there, it wouldn't be hard to get something of hers to use for that type of spell."

"Okay, then. We'll hire a private investigator right away and see if we can find proof that she hired someone." Lorna sat back in her chair and shook her head. "I wish I could say this case is unusual, but in my experience, once someone files a custody suit, the gloves have come off. The best thing to do is to remain rational and let the judge determine for themselves that the other party is the one being unreasonable."

Brody sucked in a sharp breath. "That's not easy to do when your child's future is on the line."

"I know, Brody," the lawyer said. "Trust me. I know. But if we get a decent judge, this case won't go anywhere and you can put all of this behind you."

"Only if I can shake this ghost," Zya said.

"We will." Levi walked over and stood on the other side of Zya.

Brody looked at the people in the room and realized that even though he hadn't been in Keating Hollow for long, he'd already found a circle of people he could count on. And that was more than he'd found in over five years of living in France. There was no doubt that relocating to Keating Hollow had been the best decision he'd made in a long, long time.

"Lorna, what's your take on my case? Do you think that's going to be the end of it, or will the sheriff pursue it?" Zya asked.

"I doubt it's going any further, Zya," Lorna said. "I obviously can't promise anything, but with Miss Maple refusing to cooperate, there really isn't much of a case. And since she is fine, there's not a lot of pressure to make a stand on anything. Try not to worry unless there's something to worry about."

"That's what my grandmother used to say," Zya said with a weak smile. "I'll try."

"And what about the custody case? Will my mother's threats hurt her?" Brody asked.

"If we can convince the judge that she made them, yes. That's why I want to hire a PI immediately. Keep any written communication from your parents, including email. Write down any conversations you have with her. But like I said, it's better to stop communication altogether until we have this settled. If she wants to communicate with you, she can do it through me."

"Good. I don't want to talk to her anyway." Brody stood and held out his hand to Zya. She slipped her fingers through his and held on tightly.

Zya got to her feet. "Thank you, Lorna. You've been invaluable today."

"Just doing my job." She walked them to the door. "You guys have a quiet evening. I'll get in touch when I find out anything more." Lorna nodded to Levi. "And thank you. Without you, this day would've turned out very differently."

A shudder ran through Brody's body. If Levi hadn't been there, he'd have lost Zya. Brody owed the young man more than he could ever repay.

"There's nothing to thank me for," Levi said. "I was just doing what anyone would."

Brody doubted that. Most people liked to stick to their own business. He clasped Levi on the shoulder and said, "You're one of a kind, Levi."

The young rock star snorted as if he thought that was a joke, but then he gave Brody a quick nod of acknowledgment before the three of them exited the office.

CHAPTER 21

*Z*ya clung to Brody. They were standing on her front porch with an overnight bag at her feet. If everything went the way she planned, she'd be back the next day, but there was no way to know if she'd be successful in banishing the spirit that was still following her around. She pulled back and stared up into his handsome face. "Give Winnie hugs and kisses for me."

He brushed a lock of hair out of her eyes. "I don't want to let you go."

"I don't want to go," she said.

There was no reason to hash out why she had to leave. Neither of them would put Winnie in danger.

Zya pressed up onto her tiptoes and kissed him one last time before she turned around and met Levi at her Jeep.

Brody stood on her porch, watching as she turned her Jeep around and disappeared down the driveway.

"Thank you," Zya said to Levi. "I hope I'm not too much of an imposition."

"You're not." Levi stared at his phone, frowning. Then he

tapped out a message. "Looks like my plans just got canceled anyway."

Zya turned down the main highway and headed west toward the home Levi shared with Silas. "What happened?"

"Silas isn't going to make it." He let out a sigh and turned to stare out the window. "Work schedule conflict."

"I'm sorry. I'm sure it's hard with the two of you both having such demanding careers."

"Yeah. Hard." Levi turned and stared out the window.

Zya knew when someone was done with a conversation, so she let it go. "Do you want to get takeout? I'm starving."

"Sure."

They stopped at the Keating Hollow Brewery, got burgers and fries to go, and then headed to the house that was situated on the side of the mountain.

"Levi, this is really gorgeous," Zya said when she parked in front of the modern structure. It had large plate-glass windows that looked out over the valley and had mature redwoods behind it.

"It's actually Silas's place," he said flatly as he unlocked the door.

"But you live here, too," Zya said.

"When I'm in town." He led them inside, flipping on lights as he went. "Let's eat in the kitchen."

Zya dropped her bag near the front door and hurried after him.

Levi grabbed a couple of beers and met her at the table. After handing her one, he raised the bottle in a mock toast. "To a quieter evening."

"Hear, hear." She raised her bottle and then took a long, satisfying swig.

They were quiet as they tucked into their burgers and fries.

It wasn't until Levi set his half-eaten burger down that he spoke. "The spirit hasn't been with us since we left the sheriff's office."

"That's good, but he's probably just biding his time." Zya picked at her fries. "Spirits only have so much energy. After what he did to me, it's no surprise he hasn't materialized yet."

"Is it normal for you to see spirits?" he asked.

"Yes." She smirked. "It's one of my 'gifts.' It's not fun, but I can cast spells that strengthen my barriers so they can't bother me. I doubt that's going to be enough for this one, though. I'll need to consult my grimoire to see how to banish him for good."

"Your grimoire?" he asked, his eyebrows raised.

"That sounded very witchy, didn't it?" She chuckled. "It belonged to my aunt and she left it to me. Salem witches have a long history of developing protection spells. I'm sure you have no trouble understanding why."

"No. No trouble at all." He took another sip of beer. "What was it like growing up there?"

"Honestly? It was sort of intense. So much of the focus was on being a witch instead of being a person first. My family owns an herbal business, many of them infused with magic. So it was just everywhere. Plus, my aunts like to haunt me. Here in Keating Hollow, sure, the town is magical and there are witches everywhere, but it feels different. Not weighed down by a sad history. Instead, people use their magic, but it's not the focus. It's people first, magic second. Except for now, I guess. Brody and I seem to have brought that darker side of magic with us."

"You didn't bring it with you. It followed you. Trust me. It's not the first time." He stared down at his plate before glancing up. "I had some troubles not long after I moved here with

Hope. My father was not a good person. My mother isn't much better."

"I'm sorry, Levi. You deserve better."

"So do you and Brody. At least you two have each other. As for me, I got Hope and Chad out of the deal." He grinned.

"And when you came here, you met Silas," she said helpfully.

"Yeah." His smile vanished, and Zya wanted to kick herself for bringing him up.

"Maybe you can go visit Silas instead since he can't come here?"

Levi's jaw tightened. "I would have, but Silas is being vague about his schedule, so…" He shrugged. "It's fine. I haven't spent much time with Hope lately and I'd really like to get to know Frankie better."

He most certainly wasn't fine, but Zya didn't want to push the conversation. Long distance was always a challenge. She was certain he and Silas would work it out as soon as they found some time to spend together.

Zya picked up their plates and moved to the sink to do their dishes. She had just finished loading when she glanced out the window and spotted a familiar friend. Grinning, she said, "Levi, come here. There's someone you need to meet."

Levi, who'd been rummaging around in the freezer, poked his head out and asked, "There's someone here?"

"Yes. Sort of." She waved for him to join her at the back door before she stepped out onto the porch.

The wolf sat perfectly still at the edge of the tree line, watching her.

"That's Silver," she said.

"Friend of yours?" he asked.

She nodded. "We met not too long after I moved here to

Keating Hollow. He walks with me every morning while I center myself in the woods. I think of him as a protector."

Levi studied the wolf and then nodded slowly. "Yes, I think that's exactly what he is. It's interesting that he knew how to find you."

"It is. Honestly, I'm not that surprised to see him. He did that after I moved from the inn to my house, too. It's like he just knows and then follows."

"That sounds like a really special relationship, Zya." Levi squeezed her arm and then walked back into the house.

Zya crouched down and put her hand out. The wolf immediately trotted over to her, sniffed her fingers, and then placed his head just under her hand, waiting for her to pet him.

"You're a good boy, Silver," Zya said, giving him the attention he demanded. "I have to admit, I do feel safer having you watch over me."

He leaned his entire body against her legs and let out a soft whine before he suddenly stiffened and then bolted off the porch.

Zya cried out when she spotted the spirit that had possessed her earlier. He was at the tree line, just watching them. The wolf snarled and lunged for him just as the spirit vanished into thin air.

"Zya?" Levi said, suddenly by her side. "What is it?"

She pointed toward the wolf, who was pacing the tree line, still snarling. "The spirit was there. Silver chased him away."

"Where? Out here?"

"Yes, right where Silver is now. He vanished when Silver went after him."

Levi put an arm around her shoulders. "It's okay. Come on. Let's go inside. He won't come near you with me here. Bring the wolf, too."

Zya called to Silver, but he continued to patrol the area where the spirit had been. "Looks like he's not interested."

"That's okay. He's just trying to keep you safe." Levi tugged her inside and led her toward the couch.

"Wait. I'm going to get my grimoire. I'll be right back." She couldn't continue to live her life as if she needed a bodyguard. The sooner she found a way to banish the spirit, the sooner she could move home. After rummaging around in her overnight bag, she found the book and then curled up on the other end of the couch with Levi.

His phone kept pinging with texts. It was obvious he was upset as he furiously typed his responses, but Zya didn't say anything, preferring to let him have his privacy.

She delved into the grimoire, flipping page after page, looking for a spell that would banish the spirit. By the time she was almost three-quarters of the way through it, she started to get discouraged. There were spells for protecting herself, but none that would banish a dangerous spirit.

"Seriously!" Levi cried as he jumped to his feet, gaping at his phone. "Silas said they were filming tonight." He turned his phone so that Zya could see the headline.

Silas Ansell caught on camera, dancing at local gay hangout. And that hottie dancing with him isn't Levi Kelley. Is there trouble in paradise???

"Oh, Levi. I'm sorry," Zya said, feeling terrible for him. "Maybe it isn't what it seems?" Surely he knew that gossip sites couldn't be trusted.

"He's definitely at that bar. One of his costars posted a picture of them on Instagram." Levi ran a hand through his hair and stalked into the other room, his phone pressed to his ear. A moment later, she heard him say, "What the hell, Silas?"

Zya, desperately wanting to give him some privacy,

grabbed her book and her bag and made her way to the guest room. She closed the door and finished flipping through the grimoire. Just as she was certain she was going to come up empty handed, she spotted it. A spell to cast out an undesirable spirit. She quickly scanned it and sighed in relief when she saw the spell was based in water magic. If anything was going to work, it was a spell that drew on water.

Once she was certain she had the spell memorized, she shut the book and picked up her phone. It wasn't long after Winnie's bedtime, and she hoped she'd catch Brody before he called it a night. She hit the button for Facetime and waited.

"Hey, gorgeous," Brody said when he answered.

Zya grinned at him. "Hey, yourself. I miss you."

"I miss you, too." Brody told her all about his evening with Winnie and she told him about the wolf and the spell she found.

"I'll try it in the morning," Zya said.

"I'll go with you. I'll meet you here after I drop off Winnie."

"Good deal." They spent the next hour talking about nothing important until Winnie came in and crawled in next to her father.

"I'll let you go," Zya said, ignoring the ache in her chest. She was supposed to be there with them both. She crossed her fingers, sending up a silent prayer that tomorrow she'd be back where she belonged.

"Good night, Zy," Brody said.

"Night, Zy," Winnie echoed.

Zya's heart swelled with love. "Goodnight to both of you. Have a good sleep. Love you."

In unison, they both said, "Love you, too."

Zya ended the call and hugged her phone to her chest. Even after a hellish day, she couldn't think of a better way to end it.

CHAPTER 22

"Y ou're quiet," Zya said to Levi as they walked into her house the next morning. Brody wasn't back from taking Winnie to school, so they were going in for coffee while they waited. "Is everything okay?"

"No." Levi followed her into the kitchen and leaned against the counter. "Can I ask you something?"

"Sure." She busied herself setting up the coffee pot and waited for him to continue.

"What would you do if you hadn't seen your boyfriend in over six months?"

She turned to glance at Levi. His brows were pinched and his eyes were focused on the wall behind her. "I guess it depends on the reason. You both have demanding jobs. I'm sure it isn't easy to line them up."

"True." He rubbed at his jawline. "Silas was supposed to spend these two weeks with me here. We've only seen each other a handful of times this last year, and the last time I saw him it was for all of twelve hours before I had to hop back on a plane to get to my next gig. Do you know the reason he isn't here right now?"

She shook her head then said, "Work?"

"Yeah. Work. A job he booked last minute when he was supposed to be getting on a plane to see me," Levi scoffed.

"Did he say why he booked it last minute?" she asked, wondering if it was an opportunity he just couldn't pass up.

Levi made a jerking motion with his shoulder. "No. I didn't ask. The thing is, I didn't even have to ask. I'm sure it was with some director or lead actor or producer that he thinks he needs to impress. So once again, he put his career first over us. I'm just done. I can't do it anymore."

Zya stared at him, her mouth open in shock. "You're done? Like for good?"

There were tears in his eyes as he nodded. "It's too hard, Zya. I can't do this anymore."

She reached out and took his hand in hers, squeezing it for support. There wasn't anything to say. Not really. Levi had made his choice. A very painful one. It broke her heart to hear the news. The pair had always seemed so happy together in interviews and various television appearances during the rare times they were interviewed together. It was a shame they hadn't been able to work it out.

"Is it so wrong to want to be someone's priority?" Levi asked, his voice cracking.

"No, Levi. It isn't."

"I turned down an appearance on a late night show this week to be here. It's not like I don't understand the temptation to show up for all the opportunities. But Silas was more important. I guess he doesn't feel the same."

They were silent as the coffee machine gurgled.

Finally Zya said, "This calls for Danishes." She pulled a box out of the cupboard and silently thanked Brody for not eating them all. "Here. Eat this."

Levi started to shake his head.

Zya placed her hands on her hips and said, "Come on. Sugar is a good distraction."

He gave her a halfhearted smile and took one of the Danishes.

"Good. Now, how about that coffee?"

By the time Brody walked in, they had devoured the rest of the Danishes and were on their second cup of coffee. He walked over to Zya and hugged her from behind as he kissed her on the cheek. "Ready to kick some spirit butt?"

"Definitely." She glanced at Levi. "Are you ready?"

He nodded once and then rose and cleaned up their mugs and the pastry box.

"I really like having him around," Zya said to Brody.

"I like that, too, but because he keeps you safe, not because he does dishes." Brody held his hand out to Levi. "Seriously, thanks, man."

Levi shook his head. "My pleasure. Let's go. I want to see this spell in action."

The three of them walked out the back door.

Zya wasn't at all surprised when she spotted the wolf waiting for her. He trotted to her side and together they made the familiar walk down to the lagoon.

Once they cleared the trees and the lagoon came into view, Levi stopped in his tracks. "There's more than one spirit here."

"I'm not at all surprised," Zya said, spotting both her aunts and her grandfather. They were waiting for her down by the water's edge.

"What does that mean?" Levi asked as he hurried after her.

"Zya is always seeing ghosts," Brody said. "This is where she comes to strengthen her guards so that they can't overwhelm her. If they need to talk to her, they often wait here because it takes less energy for her to come to them."

"That implies she knows them," Levi said.

"She does. They are her family," Brody explained.

"Levi," Zya called, waving her hand. "Come over here. I'll introduce you."

Levi stood next to Zya and scanned the area. At first Zya wasn't sure he saw them but then his head jerked to the right and he blinked as if he couldn't believe what he was seeing.

Zya laughed. "They're sisters. Seems unlikely, right?"

"Nah," he said with a chuckle. "They might not look anything alike, but they're both wearing the same facial expression and neither is happy."

He was right about that. Helen was tall and thin with long white hair, while Vera was short and curvy with lavender hair. But they were both scowling with their brows pinched, and they both had their arms crossed over their chests, staring at Zya in disapproval.

They're a little put out, Zya's grandfather said, suddenly appearing beside her.

"It's because I wouldn't let them bully me into dating random people from Keating Hollow," Zya said.

Charles was a lovely man, Helen called.

Zya matched her stance, crossing her arms over her chest. "He's already sweet on someone else."

So? You didn't have to cast me out just because I was trying to help.

Zya let out an exaggerated sigh. "Well, you don't have to worry anymore because Brody and I are now together. That should make you both happy."

Brody slipped his arm around her waist as if to prove that they were indeed a couple.

Both of them dropped their arms and stared at Zya in surprise. Then Vera clasped her hands together. *You and Brody finally figured it out! Yes!*

Helen started to move toward Zya, but then stopped and turned around as if she felt something behind her.

Or someone.

You're not welcome here! she cried.

He's bound to Zya, her grandfather explained. *The only way to get rid of him is to cast a spell using the blood of the person who bound them together.*

"What?" Zya's breath caught. "If that's true, we're not going to be able to get rid of him today." That spell she'd found would be useless.

You could use the blood of a relative. Her grandfather glanced at Brody then smiled down at her just before he disappeared into the ether.

"Brody," she whispered.

"Yes, love." He wrapped his arm around her waist, holding her to him. "What is it?"

"I'm pretty sure we're going to need your blood."

He raised both eyebrows. "Am I going to be the sacrificial lamb, so to speak?"

"Something like that. My aunt says that spirit is bound to me and the only way to break the spell is to use the blood of the person who cast it. Or the blood of a relative. If your mother did this, your blood would work."

Brody's facial expression hardened. "Let's do it."

"I guess we'll know for sure one way or another if your mom did this," Zya said, leaning into him.

"I guess so. Let's get started." Brody took a step back to stand near Levi, giving Zya space.

Her two aunts flanked her on both sides.

"Are you ready, Zya?" Helen asked.

"I'm ready." Zya took a step forward so that she was standing in the water. Magic flowed over her skin easily, making her feel almost invincible.

Call him to the water, Vera said. *Refer to him as your bound spirit.*

Zya did as she was told, raising her arms in the air and calling, "Spirit who is bound to me, reveal yourself!"

The tall man in the trench coat appeared briefly in the center of the lagoon, his face twisted as if he were fighting the spell tooth and nail.

Again, Helen ordered.

Zya chanted the command over and over, only stopping when the spirit stayed visible and suspended over the middle of the lagoon. The magic was draining her, and it took a moment to realize it wasn't her magic but the magic of the spirit that was bound to her. The only thing that kept her conscious was the water lapping at her feet, continuously refilling her power well.

That's it, Vera called. *Tell Brody it's time for his sacrifice!*

Zya did as her aunt said, and a moment later, Brody was by her side. Before she knew what was happening, he slit a gash in his palm and closed his fist, waiting for the next order.

Good, Vera said, nodding. *Zya, repeat after me. When spirits are bound, freedom is lost. Break the chains. Pay the cost. Unbind my soul. One of two and two of three, be gone unwelcome spirit, so mote it be!*

Zya called out the command, using every ounce of her energy she could muster. As soon as the first two lines left her lips, the spirit let out an animalistic growl and flew directly at her. Zya stood taller, never faltering as she called out the next line, "Break the chains!"

The spirit twisted in on himself, contorting as if he were being tortured.

"Pay the cost. Unbind the soul!"

Silver started running back and forth, his teeth bared.

"One of two and two of three," Zya continued.

The spirit shot from his spot, aiming for Zya.

She opened her mouth to finish the spell, but Silver jumped in front of her, intercepting the connection with the spirit and causing him to turn to dust and fall to the ground.

Zya wanted to ask what the hell just happened, but she knew better than to disrupt a spell, so she grabbed Brody's bloody hand and finished the incantation. "Be gone unwelcome spirit." She turned Brody's hand over so that the blood would drip into her palm. "So mote it be!"

The wind picked up, blowing Zya's hair back and causing the lagoon to ripple from the powerful force. Then suddenly it was calm. Completely calm without even a flicker of weather.

The dust of the spirit that was scattered on the ground rose into the air and re-formed into the tall man in the trench coat, and he snarled at Zya.

Zya opened her palm and let a few drops of Brody's blood drop into the water.

Storm clouds appeared overhead, and suddenly rain poured down just over the lagoon, soaking them to the bone. Lightning flickered once, and then five bolts came from nowhere, lighting up the spirit. He twisted and turned and contorted, trying to break free. But then suddenly he burst into flames, and when the ashes started to fall, the wind swept them up into the storm cloud just before it vanished, leaving them standing under the morning blue skies.

He's gone, Helen said.

Zya turned to Brody, finding his face ashen. She quickly slipped her arms around him. "I'm sorry, Brody."

"It's true. My mother did this to you." His speech was stilted as he spoke. "She ordered a spirit to possess you. And if that didn't work, he was supposed to kill you. She wanted to destroy the woman I love."

Zya held him tighter. "I'm okay, Brody. I promise."

He stroked one hand down her hair. "I know, Zya. But am I?"

hen they got back to the house, Levi shoved his hands into his pockets and said, "I guess that's it then." He gave Zya a wry smile. "You don't need me as your bodyguard anymore."

Brody, overwhelmed with appreciation, held out his hand to the singer. "Thank you, man. There's nothing I can say to express how grateful I am for your help. Our door is always open to you. I hope you know that."

Levi shook his hand. "No thanks required. I'm just glad Zya's ancestors were able to help her find a solution. And I'm sorry about your mom. I'm no stranger to messed-up parental relationships. It's just all kinds of wrong."

"Agreed." Brody pulled him into a half-hug, thumping him on the back the way men often did to show appreciation. In his mind, Levi Kelley would always be family.

After Brody released Levi, Zya walked over to him and gave him a big hug. "Thank you, Levi. I wouldn't be here without you. I don't know how I'll ever repay you."

He shook his head. "There's nothing to repay. I'm just glad I could help."

"Call me if you need anything," Zya said. "Even if it's just to talk. Okay?"

"Sure." Levi nodded at her and then headed for the door. Before he pulled it open, he turned around and chuckled softly. "Uh, could one of you give me a ride? Zya and I came in her Jeep."

"Sure." Brody grabbed his keys and turned to Zya. "I'll be right back."

"I'll be here." She kissed him softly on the lips.

Suddenly all Brody wanted to do was sweep her up in his arms and carry her to the bedroom. Reluctantly, he stepped away and turned to Levi. "Let's go."

THE MOMENT BRODY stepped through the door after dropping off Levi, he pulled Zya into his arms and buried his face in her neck.

She automatically wrapped her arms around him and then slid her fingers up his neck and into his hair. "It's okay now," she soothed. "The spirit is gone. Blair won't be able to bind him to me again."

He just wasn't able to comprehend the fact that his mother had done something so heinous. Did she hate Zya that much, or was she just so controlling that she thought if she could remove Zya from his life he'd just come running home?

Controlling. He let out a snort. More like insane. Who in their right mind did things like that?

"Brody?" Zya gently pulled back and met his gaze.

"I'm fine," he lied. He didn't want to talk about his mother.

All he wanted was to lose himself in Zya's arms and forget everything that had happened in the last twenty-four hours. He lowered his head and brushed a gentle kiss over her lips. His heart fluttered, something that had never happened to him before when he was kissing anyone. He broke the kiss and smiled against her lips. "This is even better than I imagined."

She chuckled. "You've barely even kissed me, Brody."

"True. But I can already tell you're going to ruin me for anyone else."

"I hope you know there's not ever going to be anyone else," she shot back.

Brody grinned. "You're staking your claim, are you?"

"Damn right I am." She lifted up onto her tiptoes, covering his mouth with hers.

He loved the way she tasted. Her sweetness and unmistakable desire. She wanted him. That was clear. But he didn't just want her; he *needed* her. But there was something else he needed first. Gently, he stepped back, holding her at her waist.

"What's wrong?" she asked.

"Nothing's wrong." He caressed her cheek with his thumb. "There's just something we need to get straight before we go any further."

Worry flickered in her gaze. "Okay. What is it?"

He took a deep breath. "I need you to promise me you won't run if and when things get rough. Because we know they will eventually. If not with my parents, then someday when Winnie's processing the fact that she lost her mother. Life is messy, and if we're in this, then I want us to be in it 100%. No more thinking you have to sacrifice yourself for me or Winnie. You're just as important to this family."

She bit down on her lower lip and averted her gaze. When

she finally spoke, she said, "I know I ran from Salem and my family. From that mess with Carter. And I've run from other relationships, too. But you and Winnie? You're different. You know that, right?"

He nodded, because he did know. But that didn't change the fact that she'd told him more than once that she'd leave to protect him and Winnie. "I do. But I need to know you're not going to run, no matter the reason. Zy, baby, I love you so much. Let me keep loving you through it all. The good, the bad, and the ugly. Because this is it for me. Do you understand what I'm saying?"

"I do." There were tears in her eyes as she added, "The same goes for you as well, Brody Saxon. You've done your share of running, too. I need to know that when our relationship hits a rough patch you won't give up on us so you can move on to something easier. Someone who requires less commitment."

That was an easy one. He smiled down at her. "Don't you know by now that the reason I couldn't commit to any of those other women is because none of them were you? Like I said, I'm in this. All the way. Are you?"

"Yes," she said with a definitive nod. "All the way. No matter what."

"Good. Now come here so I can kiss you." All thoughts of the past twenty-four hours fled his mind. The only thing that mattered was the gorgeous girl in his arms whom he'd loved since he was a boy.

Finally, he thought. She was what he'd been waiting for all those years.

"Brody," she said breathlessly a few moments later, "I want you."

That was all he needed to hear. In one swift movement, he lifted her up into his arms. Her legs went around him and then she was kissing him again. He was tempted to just press her up against the wall, to explore her right there in her living room, but he'd been dreaming about this moment for far too long. He was going to savor every second of it.

Walking slowly but deliberately, he carried her down the hallway and into her bedroom. One of her hands was in his hair and the other was clutching his backside. He could have stood there like that forever, but his fingers ached to touch her everywhere.

"Zy, I need you out of these clothes," he said huskily as he set her on her feet.

She reached down to tug at the hem of her shirt. Then with her eyes locked on his, she tore it off, leaving her standing there in a pretty red-lace bra. Her skin was perfect. Smooth and slightly sun-kissed.

"Holy hell, Zy. You're going to kill me, aren't you?"

"If I do, it'll be one hell of a way to go, don't you think?" Her nimble fingers made quick work of his shirt and then she moved on to relieve him of his jeans. When he was just in his boxer briefs, she stood back, admiring him. Her gaze devoured him, taking in every inch.

Brody couldn't help it. He took the opportunity to flex his pecs.

Zya threw her head back and laughed. Then she reached out and ran her hand along his chest and over one of his nipples. "You just had to show off, didn't you?"

"You seemed to be enjoying the show. I thought I'd give you a little bonus content." He winked at her and then stepped in close, kissing her again.

Zya melted into him, her skin warm and so soft that he never wanted to stop touching her.

"I need more of you," he said, moving to kiss her neck as he

215

finished undressing her. When she was bared to him, he lost the ability to speak. She was a goddess. Everything about her was perfect.

"Your turn," she said, her voice low and full of desire. Then her hands were on his waist, tugging his briefs down.

Brody started to tremble with unchecked need. He felt like he was a teenager and this was his first time. He supposed it was since he'd never been with anyone he'd loved before.

Zya sat on the bed and tugged him down with her until he was covering her body.

"I love you, Zya," he said, propping himself up on his elbows as he stroked her hair.

"I know, Brody. I love you, too."

Then their lips met and magic sparked between them as they got lost in each other.

BRODY WOKE with Zya curled up next to him. They'd spent hours exploring each other that morning. He hadn't been satisfied until he'd learned every last inch of her body. He'd known he loved her before, but now that they'd shared their most intimate sides with each other, he knew he'd never survive it if anything ever happened to her.

As content as he was, he couldn't keep the dark events of the past twenty-four hours from creeping in. He was still in shock that his mother had done such an awful thing to Zya just to try to maintain control over her only son. The slow boil of rage churned in his gut.

He glanced over at Zya. She had a little smile on her face and was sleeping so peacefully it made his heart squeeze with affection. Dammit, his heart felt like it was going to explode from emotion. Rolling over, Brody gave her a soft kiss on the cheek and then rose from her bed.

Their bed. He'd already moved his stuff into her room after explaining to Winnie the night before that he and Zya would be roommates from now on. She'd taken the new situation in stride, just as he'd suspected she would. And then she'd turned her attention to PJ, her favorite stuffed animal, while he'd hung his clothes in an underused section of Zya's closet.

After taking a quick shower and throwing on fresh jeans and a T-shirt, Brody snuck out of the room, left Zya a note on the kitchen counter, and then headed across town. He had things to discuss with his mother. He knew Lorna had told him not to speak with her, but he just couldn't let this go. His own mother had betrayed him in an unforgivable way and keeping silent just wasn't an option. He had to hear what she had to say for herself.

When he arrived at the inn, he stood outside his mother's room and tried his best to get his anger under control. He had things to say, and if he did it in a rage-induced stupor, this meeting would be useless. He was just about to knock when the door swung open.

His mother's eyes widened in surprise and then her expression turned blank as she said, "Brody. I wasn't expecting you."

He glanced down at the bags near her feet and then strode in without an invitation. Turning to glare at her, he asked, "Were you going somewhere?"

She cleared her throat. "As a matter of fact, I was. Since you have no interest in working out our differences, I decided to go back to Salem until the custody hearing."

"There isn't going to be a custody hearing, Mother. Not

after the crap you pulled." He was leaning against an armoire, just watching her.

His mother swallowed, a sure sign that she was nervous. "I don't know what you're talking about, Brody."

He raised one eyebrow. "Oh, you don't? You don't remember casting a binding spell to a Saxon spirit and then ordering him to terrorize Zya?"

Surprise flashed in her ice blue eyes before it vanished. "What makes you say such an absurd thing? Isn't it obvious that Zya isn't well? Surely you aren't blaming me for the trouble she caused yesterday. Brody, that's just delusional."

"Is it?" He held up his palm, showing her the still tender wound where he'd cut himself. "Is that why my blood sent that spirit back to hell or wherever it came from?"

She let out an audible gasp and pressed her left hand to her neck.

"Stop lying, Mother. Your manipulative tactics won't work on me. I'm willing to bet that if Dad were here, he'd have a similar wound. Am I right?"

She glanced away, unable to look at him, and he knew he'd hit the nail on the head.

"The only thing that is going to happen is that you're going to end up in jail for unlawful magic with the intent to harm," he continued. "Don't you understand? You've been found out. I'll never be your son again. It's over."

"Brody!" she cried, tears pooling in her eyes. "I didn't do it. I swear. I don't know what happened."

He scoffed. "How else would a Saxon ancestor be bound to Zya? You're the one with the magic to make the spell happen, and Dad's the one with the blood bond. Do you really expect me to believe that someone else did this? The only other person it could have been is Uncle Rodney, and he doesn't even know Zya!"

"I swear," she said, clutching at his arm. "I didn't mean for it to happen that way. I had no idea the spirit would try to harm someone else. Or go after Zya. I just wanted him to be enough of a nuisance that it would help our case when weird stuff started happening around her. I never intended for anyone to get hurt."

He wasn't sure he believed her, but at least he'd gotten a confession. Unfortunately, that didn't help at all. "Here's what's going to happen. You're going to drop the custody case. Then you're going to go back home and tell Dad exactly what you did and why I'm not going to let either of you be in Winnie's life. You can tell him if he interferes, I'll take everything I have to the police and press charges."

Her eyes narrowed and all of her remorse was gone. "You'll never make those stick."

"Maybe not," he conceded. "But it will be all over the news. Can you imagine what your country club friends will think once the entire story gets out? We have people here who will corroborate our story. What do you have? Just bravado that you can say and do anything you want without consequence. Sorry, Mother. I'm a Saxon, too. Do you think I haven't learned how to play hardball?"

"You wouldn't dare," she said, her voice full of venom.

"He wouldn't have to," a voice said from the open door. It appeared that neither of them had noticed that the door hadn't closed behind Brody.

Brody cut his gaze to Deputy Sheriff Baker. He stood with his feet shoulder width apart with his hands holding his utility belt.

"He wouldn't have to do what?" Blair Saxon asked, putting on an air of complete innocence.

"Play hardball," the deputy sheriff said. "Or press charges, because my department has that covered already. You see, Mrs. Saxon, we don't take kindly to people binding spirits to our residents here in Keating Hollow. There are assault charges on the table for what happened to Miss Maple yesterday. As well as when Zya was attacked in my office. All signs point to you as being responsible. I suggest you make peace with the media storm that's coming your way. And get a good lawyer."

Brody stood completely still, in shock that the deputy already seemed to know what was going on.

"I didn't..." his mother stammered. "I would never..." She clasped her hand over her mouth and let out a horrified cry.

"You did and you would," the sheriff said. "I think your son is right. You should drop that custody case immediately. Or else there's going to be an ugly criminal case that you won't be able to run away from."

"I... what?" she asked, her eyes wide with fear.

Drew Baker strode into the room and stopped right in front of Blair Saxon. "I think you heard me, but let me be clear. Drop that custody case against your son, and there's a good chance these charges go away."

"Um, okay. Yes. I can do that," she said.

"Do it now. Call your lawyer. Have him send a confirmation to my office immediately," Drew ordered.

Brody was in complete shock. Why was the deputy sheriff battling this for him? It wasn't like he really even knew Drew Baker. Nonetheless, he was extremely grateful for the help.

His mother did as she was told. Once she was on the phone with her lawyer, it became clear that he'd never really been on board with the case but had taken it because Brody's parents were longtime clients.

"I know it was a waste of time and resources," his mother said into the phone, irritated. "Like I told you last time, that was never my concern. Just drop the custody suit. My son is fully capable of taking care of his daughter."

When she ended the call, she turned to Drew. "It's done. What assurances do I have that this matter is settled?"

"None," he said, glaring at her. "Just my word. Leave town now, or our deal is off. Understand?"

His mother clenched her fists, obviously fuming that he dared speak to her in such a manner. Blair turned to her son. "I hope we can move past this, Brody. Winnie is only young for a short time. I want to be a part of her life."

"You destroyed that chance when you went after Zya," he said, holding firm. "Go home, Mother. You're done here."

Blair Saxon stared at him for a long moment and then spun on her heel. After grabbing her bags, she stalked out of the room, her head held high as if she hadn't just narrowly avoided being arrested.

After she disappeared into the elevator, Drew Baker shut the door to her hotel room and turned to Brody. "I'm sorry for the way everything went down yesterday."

Brody shook his head. "It's not your fault. But how did you figure out it was my mother behind the spirit binding?"

The deputy sheriff gave Brody a half smile. "Did you know that lagoon is on Wanda Danvers's property?"

"I think I did know that. Why?"

"She was there this morning when Zya broke the spell. She saw everything and came straight to me. The truth is, I really did want to arrest your mother. What she did is both dangerous and illegal here in Keating Hollow. But we only have circumstantial evidence, and I'm not sure it was enough to even hold her. Especially with the kind of lawyers she employs. So I decided to try to help you out instead. I find that most people of your mother's economic and social status cave pretty easily when there's a prospect of seeing even a few moments of jail time."

Brody was stunned into silence. Instead of saying anything, he stepped forward and wrapped the man in a hug.

The deputy sheriff stiffened at first, clearly surprised, but then chuckled softly and hugged him back.

Brody quickly released him. "Sorry, man. You just have no idea what a relief it is to have this matter settled. I don't know how to thank you. Can I take you out for a beer sometime?"

"There's no need to thank me," Drew said, waving a dismissive hand. "That's just my job. But I'll gladly take you up on that beer sometime." He handed Brody a business card. "Call me and we'll make it happen."

"I will."

The deputy sheriff tipped his hat to Brody and disappeared, leaving Brody in the room, still stunned at the turn of events.

As if on cue, his phone rang, showing a picture of Zya. He quickly answered it and said, "You're never going to guess what just happened."

CHAPTER 24

"*Y*ou got Winnie her own golf cart?" Zya exclaimed as she jumped out of her Jeep and strode over to Brody. He'd closed on his house a month ago, and ever since then, they'd been busy renovating and getting the land ready to plant grapes. It was nowhere near ready for them to move in, but the back patio had been completed and they were hosting a barbeque for their friends.

"Do you think it's too much?" Brody asked, his eyes twinkling with mischief.

Zya glanced at the two matching gold carts that sat next to each other in front of the garage and shook her head. "You're going to spoil that girl senseless."

He threw his head back and laughed.

"What?" Zya demanded. "How is that funny?"

"It's not for Winnie, my love. It's for you." He grabbed her hand and led her over to the matching gold carts. On the back they said *His* and *Hers*. "Mine is for tooling around the property and yours is for… well, whatever you want. I hear there's a group of women who really enjoy a good golf cart race every now and then."

"Hell yeah, we do!" Wanda called from her spot near the porch.

Zya stared at the golf carts and then at Brody. Shaking her head, she slipped her arms around him and said, "You're a little bit nuts. You know that, right? I'm sure just one golf cart would've been fine."

"Nope." He shook his head. "I was told you needed your own." He nodded toward Wanda. "And to expect for it to be souped-up before the end of the month."

Wanda waved at Zya and nodded vigorously.

Winnie jumped in the one marked *Hers* and grabbed the wheel. "Let's go, Zya!"

"Looks like you've been summoned," Brody said and kissed her on the top of the head.

"You know that's going to be a thing now, right? Every time we come out here, I'm going to have to take her tooling around the property."

"Is that a bad thing?" he asked with one eyebrow raised.

"No." Zya chuckled. "Just wanted you to be aware that means less help from me since I'll be playing chauffeur. In fact, this might be the best present ever now that I don't have to scrape popcorn ceilings or deal with old wallpaper."

"I'm just looking out for you, babe." He pulled her into a sideways hug and added, "Have fun, you two."

Zya climbed into the golf cart, knowing she had a goofy grin on her face, and watched as Drew Baker approached Brody and handed him a beer. The two had become really good friends ever since the day Drew had forced Blair Saxon's hand and she'd dropped the lawsuit. Zya was glad. Brody had settled into Keating Hollow and had easily become part of the fabric of the town in such a short time.

"This way, Zya!" Wanda called, rolling up next to her in her own souped-up golf cart. She sped off, the music blaring from her purple ride.

"Go, Zya!" Winnie demanded, and Zya stepped on the accelerator, making the cart go all of fifteen miles an hour. They followed Wanda up over a small hill and then came to a stop where Wanda was parked along with one other cart.

"Get over here, Winnie," Yvette Townsend called. "There's a roasted marshmallow with your name on it."

A handful of Zya's friends were sitting around a firepit, roasting marshmallows and watching their kids play nearby on the swing set and jungle gym that Brody had put in for Winnie.

"There's one for you, too," Wanda said, waving Zya over to an open chair.

Zya sat next to Wanda and happily took the already roasted marshmallow. Then she glanced around at her friends. The Townsend sisters were all there along with Wanda, Hanna, and Brinn. They were all chitchatting and gossiping about upcoming birthdays, anniversaries, and... an engagement?

"Who's getting married?" Zya asked.

They all stopped talking and stared at her.

Zya blinked. "Um, guys? What's going on?"

Yvette Townsend let out a nervous laugh and said, "We're just wondering when Brinn and Austin are going to finally tie the knot."

"Oh, right," Zya said, smiling at Brinn. "When is the date?"

Brinn shrugged. "We're not in any hurry. Maybe the summer. Maybe something small down by the river."

"This summer, huh?" Zya said. "We should plan a

bachelorette party. Maybe in San Francisco? Or Napa? Just some place where we can let our hair down a little."

Everyone chimed in with their preferences for a bachelorette party, while Brinn just grinned at them, making noncommittal noises.

Zya turned to Hope, who was on her other side, and asked, "How's Levi doing?" He'd left town about a week after she'd stayed at his house. They'd had lunch and promised to keep in touch, but she hadn't heard from him despite her few texts. She was getting a little worried.

"He's okay," Hope said with a sigh. "Right now he's in the studio, working on an album of breakup songs." She frowned. "Honestly, I'm not sure he's okay at all. But Seth is keeping an eye on him and they are producing some fantastic music, so all I can do is be here for him if he wants to talk."

"Ugh. I hate that for him. Breakups are so hard."

"Yes, especially under these circumstances. They didn't break up because someone did something terrible. It was because it was just too hard to be together when both of their careers are pulling them in different directions. I just hope that one day—"

Hope was cut off suddenly when Wanda stood up and shouted, "It's time! Everyone hop in the golf carts."

"Where are we going?" Zya asked as she hurried over to Winnie and scooped her up.

"You'll see."

Winnie was absolutely giddy when they got into the golf cart. Brinn and Yvette climbed into the back seat with Skye while the rest of the women and children occupied the other carts.

"This way!" Wanda waved a hand and then took off across the field, headed away from the house.

"Where in the world is she going?" Zya asked.

Winnie giggled, but no one said anything else.

Zya glanced over at Winnie. "Is there something you're not telling me?"

The little girl closed her mouth and mimed locking it with a key.

"That's not suspicious at all," Zya said, grinning. She didn't know what was going on, but clearly Winnie did, and Zya didn't want to ruin the fun. She spent the next few minutes guessing what it might be. "Did your dad get us a pony?"

"Nope." The little girl shook her head furiously.

"Are we going swimming down at the river?"

"Too cold," Winnie insisted.

"Okay, how about... Are we looking for buried treasure?"

Winnie's eyes sparkled with interest, but she still shook her head. Zya made a point of remembering that. Maybe one day she'd make a scavenger hunt for sparkly things when they needed to fill an afternoon.

They rounded a hilly area and parked.

Zya glanced around, frowning. This was a part of the property she hadn't been to before.

"This way!" Winnie had already jumped out and rounded the golf cart. She grabbed Zya's hand and tugged. Zya stood and followed the little girl through a small patch of trees and then froze.

Brody was standing at the edge of an overlook, candles surrounding him as he looked out over the Keating Hollow river.

"Come on, Zya," Winnie said, tugging on her again.

Zya let herself be pulled forward and felt hot tears sting her eyes when Brody turned around to face her.

He had changed into dark jeans, a button-down shirt, and a

tailored blazer. The man looked like he was ready to model for the cover of *GQ*.

Zya glanced down at her skinny jeans and oversized lace tunic and wished she'd known to dress for the occasion.

Brody reached out and caressed her cheek. "You look amazing, Zya."

She stared up at him. "So do you."

"Zya," Winnie said in a shy voice.

She glanced down at the little girl standing next to her father.

Winnie reached into her dad's pocket and pulled out a small blue-velvet box and opened it, revealing a large blue sapphire. It was Zya's favorite stone.

He chuckled. "We surprised you, didn't we?" Then he got down on one knee, wrapped his arm around Winnie, and held Zya's gaze as he spoke. "Zya Rossi, Winnie and I want to know if you'd do us the honor of marrying us?"

They'd talked a little bit about getting engaged, that they wanted to be a family. But that's all it had been. Just talk. Zya had known it would happen eventually, but she hadn't expected this. That he and Winnie would propose together or that they'd do it in front of all their friends, overlooking the magical Keating Hollow river. It was everything she could've ever hoped for.

Zya knelt down in front of them, letting the tears fall unchecked down her cheeks. "Nothing would make me happier than to marry you both," she choked out and then wrapped her arms around both of them.

The small crowd that was waiting several yards away started cheering and hollering their approval.

Zya pulled back and Winnie twisted out of their embrace,

immediately running back to Yvette and Skye to excitedly tell them the news as if they hadn't just witnessed it themselves.

Zya raised her eyebrows at Brody. "That was quite the show you put on. You weren't even a little nervous about how I'd answer?"

"Actually, I was, but Winnie wasn't. She told me to man up and just ask."

"Man up?" Zya repeated as a laugh rumbled in her chest. "Where did she hear that?"

He shrugged. "School, I guess. But it turns out she was right. All I needed to do was man up, and now I'm marrying the love of my life. When are you free? Next weekend?"

Zya shook her head, unable to control the massive grin claiming her face. "I am, but if you don't mind, I'd rather wait until fall."

"Why?" he asked curiously.

"Because I want to do it here, among your new grape vines. Is that okay?"

Brody stood, pulling her with him, and then enveloped her in a hug. "Zya Rossi, you might just be the perfect woman. Yes. I'll marry you this fall, right here in our own little paradise."

CHAPTER 25

TWO YEARS LATER

Silas Ansell paced the small area of his studio apartment. He had a glass of whiskey in one hand and a script in the other. He turned and gave his sister an incredulous look. "This is seriously the best offer that came in? They're not even offering scale."

Shannon sat on his loveseat with her legs crossed and shrugged. "It is, unfortunately. The compensation is so low because they don't have a major backer yet."

He glanced at the script for a sitcom where they wanted him to play a supporting character who was a stereotypical dudebro womanizer. There wasn't much acting. He'd just pop in and say outrageous things and then leave the scene. "I can't do this. There's a better than good chance that it won't even make it to streaming."

"That's true," Shannon said. "I agree that it's not the right move for you. But you wanted to see the offers, so I brought them." His sister, who also happened to be his agent, gave him an apologetic smile. "I'm sorry, Silas. I know you were hoping for better. It's just rough right now. Studios are going through some changes and opportunities aren't really great for anyone right now who isn't locked into a series or franchise."

"It's not your fault," he said with a sigh. "I'm not blaming you. It's just frustrating."

"I know." Shannon stood and walked to the window, looking out over the small town of Befana Bay, the place he'd been living the past two years when he wasn't on location for his series *Timekeeper Academy*. It's also where he'd filmed *Witching For You,* a movie based on Miranda Moon's book, and besides Keating Hollow, it was the only place that truly felt like home. All of his costars had moved back to their hometowns or had hightailed it back to LA. But not Silas. He hated LA. And Keating Hollow... Well, he just hadn't been ready to go back. Not yet.

"You don't have to do anything. You know that, right?" Shannon said. "You have plenty of money, and eventually the big studios will come knocking again."

He did know he didn't need to do anything, but he wasn't so sure about the studios looking to hire him again. Hollywood types were far too fickle for anyone to count on that happening.

Silas Ansell was an Oscar-winning actor who'd spent the last five years proving himself in the business. He'd taken all kinds of roles, big and small, to demonstrate that he could play any character so he wouldn't be typecast as his teenage character in the hit show *Timekeeper Academy*. He'd always known the day would come when the series would be canceled, and he'd wanted options to grow. He'd witnessed too many of his costars flail after a successful show ended because no one could see them as anything other than the character they'd played for years.

But in the past six months since the show had been

canceled, the offers had been few and far between. And it was starting to worry him. "If I don't keep working, my career could stall."

"You're right. It could," Shannon agreed. "We've seen that happen before. But it's not like *Timekeeper* is your only credit. You've put in the work. I don't think it's so terrible to wait until the right role comes along."

"It's been six months, Shan!" he yelled and threw back the last of the whiskey.

She frowned at him. "I know you're anxious about your next roles, but I've never seen you like this before. What's really bothering you, Silas?"

"Besides the fact that my career has stalled?" he asked, sitting across from her and closing his eyes. "This is not how I thought things would go after the series ended."

"We always knew this was a possibility," she said gently. "I thought the plan was to just lay low for a while until you found something you could pour your heart into."

That had been the plan. But that had been back when he had a heart to give. Two years ago, his heart had been ripped out and he'd never really gotten it back. Levi's shining eyes flashed in his mind, and he quickly shoved the image aside. He hadn't seen Levi in over two years.

In those two years, Silas had done everything in his power not to think of his ex, because if he did, then he'd have to face the fact that he was the one responsible for destroying their relationship.

It was why he was taking this slump so hard. He'd sacrificed his relationship with Levi for his career. And now look at where he'd ended up. Living in a studio apartment, hundreds of miles away from the home he'd shared with Levi, all because he couldn't face going back there to an empty house.

Shannon's phone pinged with a text. She glanced at it and then read more carefully. "Si?"

"Yeah?" He pressed his fingertips to his temples, trying to combat the sudden headache.

"You just got an offer for a lead in a queer rock star romance."

His eyes popped open and he sat up. "Really? Who's the other lead?"

"Will Weeks. You know him, right?"

Silas's frustration vanished. "Yes, I know Will. He's a great guy. How are the terms?"

"Give me a minute," she said with a chuckle. "I just sent you the script. Let me look over their offer while you check it out."

Silas picked up his laptop and hurried to open the email his sister had sent. It only took reading the credits on the first page before he knew he was in. The terms didn't even matter. The movie was written by Miranda Moon and Cameron Copeland. He'd already starred in one movie for them, and if they wanted him, he was in.

IT WAS strange being back in Keating Hollow. All of Silas's memories were inundated with his time with Levi, and that made everything bittersweet. His house felt too big. He didn't like going into town because everyone knew about his relationship with Levi, and even if they didn't comment on it, they all had a sympathetic look on their faces.

It had been two years. If he and Levi had gotten over it, they could too.

The problem was Silas *hadn't* gotten over it. Not by a longshot. If it hadn't been for the film he'd signed on to do, he'd have left the day after he arrived. But he wouldn't let Miranda and Cameron down, so he was in Keating Hollow for the foreseeable future.

He pulled his sleek Tesla into a spot at the Pelsh Winery. It was the first day of production, and they were there to do a table read of the entire script before they started filming the next day. The thought settled him. If there was one thing that could get his mind off Levi, it was when he sank into a role. Working had always been Silas's salvation, and today he needed it more than ever.

It was late summer and the leaves were just about to turn on the vines, making the winery a perfect filming location. He could already see the visuals on the big screen. His skin started to buzz with anticipation.

As he walked through the barn doors where the crew was meeting, his phone chimed. He glanced down and saw that it was Shannon. The text said, *Call me now. It's important.*

Silas tapped her number and hit Send. As he was bringing the phone up to his ear, he heard a familiar voice behind him.

"Silas?"

A shiver crawled up Silas's spine as he slowly turned around. His gaze landed on the tall, lanky, yet toned body of the most beautiful man he'd ever known. "Levi? You're here."

Shannon answered the phone. "Si? Are you at the set yet?"

"Yes," he said into the phone, unable to tear his eyes away from the one man he'd ever loved.

"I just got a call. Will Weeks had an accident and had to drop out last minute. The studio cast someone new as your love interest."

He barely heard her words as he and Levi held each other's gazes, both appearing to be lost in their own thoughts.

"Silas? Are you listening? It's Levi. They cast Levi."

He blinked, then the words sank in. "You're starring in this movie?" he asked Levi.

"Oh. Em. Gee. He's right there? Silas, what's happening?" Shannon demanded.

"I'll have to call you back, sis," he said and ended the call.

Levi let out a small huff of laughter. "I'm guessing you didn't know I'd be here."

Silas shook his head.

"Would you have shown up if you did?" It was an accusation. There was no denying that.

Silas cleared his throat. "Yes, of course. I'm under contract."

"Figures. I guess I should have demanded one back when we were dating. Maybe then I wouldn't have been stood up so many times." He spun on his heel and left Silas gaping at him.

DEANNA'S BOOK LIST

Witches of Keating Hollow:
Soul of the Witch
Heart of the Witch
Spirit of the Witch
Dreams of the Witch
Courage of the Witch
Love of the Witch
Power of the Witch
Essence of the Witch
Muse of the Witch
Vision of the Witch
Waking of the Witch
Honor of the Witch
Promise of the Witch
Return of the Witch

Witches of Christmas Grove:
A Witch For Mr. Holiday
A Witch For Mr. Christmas

A Witch For Mr. Winter
A Witch For Mr. Mistletoe
A Witch For Mr. Frost

Premonition Pointe Novels:

Witching For Grace
Witching For Hope
Witching For Joy
Witching For Clarity
Witching For Moxie
Witching For Kismet

Miss Matched Midlife Dating Agency:

Star-crossed Witch
Honor-bound Witch
Outmatched Witch
Moonstruck Witch

Jade Calhoun Novels:

Haunted on Bourbon Street
Witches of Bourbon Street
Demons of Bourbon Street
Angels of Bourbon Street
Shadows of Bourbon Street
Incubus of Bourbon Street
Bewitched on Bourbon Street
Hexed on Bourbon Street
Dragons of Bourbon Street

Pyper Rayne Novels:

Spirits, Stilettos, and a Silver Bustier
Spirits, Rock Stars, and a Midnight Chocolate Bar

Spirits, Beignets, and a Bayou Biker Gang
Spirits, Diamonds, and a Drive-thru Daiquiri Stand
Spirits, Spells, and Wedding Bells

Ida May Chronicles:

Witched To Death
Witch, Please
Stop Your Witchin'

Crescent City Fae Novels:

Influential Magic
Irresistible Magic
Intoxicating Magic

Last Witch Standing:

Bewitched by Moonlight
Soulless at Sunset
Bloodlust By Midnight
Bitten At Daybreak

Witch Island Brides:

The Wolf's New Year Bride
The Vampire's Last Dance
The Warlock's Enchanted Kiss
The Shifter's First Bite

Destiny Novels:

Defining Destiny
Accepting Fate

Wolves of the Rising Sun:

Jace

Aiden

Luc

Craved

Silas

Darien

Wren

Black Bear Outlaws:

Cyrus

Chase

Cole

Bayou Springs Alien Mail Order Brides:

Zeke

Gunn

Echo

ABOUT THE AUTHOR

New York Times and USA Today bestselling author, Deanna Chase, is a native Californian, transplanted to the slower paced lifestyle of southeastern Louisiana. When she isn't writing, she is often goofing off with her husband in New Orleans or playing with her two shih tzu dogs. For more information and updates on newest releases visit her website at deannachase.com.